WITHDRAWN

WITHDRAWN

W9-CSH-914

THE CHRISTMAS SWAP

THE CHRISTMAS SWAP

MELODY CARLSON

THORNDIKE PRESS
A part of Gale, a Cengage Company

GALE
A Cengage Company

Copyright © Carlson Management Company.
Thorndike Press, a part of Gale, a Cengage Company.

ALL RIGHTS RESERVED
This book is a work of fiction. Names, characters, places, and incidents are the product of the author's imagination or are used fictitiously. Any resemblance to actual events, locales, or persons, living or dead, is coincidental.
Thorndike Press® Large Print Christian Fiction.
The text of this Large Print edition is unabridged.
Other aspects of the book may vary from the original edition.
Set in 16 pt. Plantin.

LIBRARY OF CONGRESS CIP DATA ON FILE.
CATALOGUING IN PUBLICATION FOR THIS BOOK
IS AVAILABLE FROM THE LIBRARY OF CONGRESS.

ISBN-13: 978-1-4328-8442-0 (hardcover alk. paper)

Published in 2020 by arrangement with Revell Books, a division of Baker Publishing Group

Printed in Mexico
Print Number: 01   Print Year: 2020

THE CHRISTMAS SWAP

ONE

Emma Daley had always loved Christmas as a child, but . . . not so much as an adult. That was probably because she'd been spending Christmas with her best friend Gillian's family ever since her parents moved to the other side of the planet. Christmas at the Landerses' opulent Scottsdale home meant fabulous food, fancy clothes, expensive gifts — at least from them. Emma couldn't afford that kind of extravagance. And of course, the holidays were never complete without the usual Landers family feud.

It wasn't that Emma didn't appreciate Gillian's family, or their hospitality, but sometimes she longed for something more . . . or maybe it was something less. So this year Emma had decided to do it differently. She planned to spend her holidays alone. And that was what she'd just told Gillian.

"I haven't spent Christmas at home since

my parents left," Emma explained as the two met for coffee. It was the same coffeehouse they'd frequented as ASU college freshmen fourteen years ago. And the same town Emma had grown up in and where she now made her meager living as a substitute English teacher. "I think it'll be fun to spend Christmas in Tempe."

"Fun? To be alone? You can't be serious." Gillian set her cup down with a clunk.

"I know it probably sounds weird, but it's what I want, and I plan to get a real tree and make a fire in the fireplace — just like Dad would do. Even if it's eighty degrees outside."

"But you don't understand, Em. You *have* to spend Christmas with us," Gillian insisted.

"Not this year." Emma looked down at her steaming latte, trying to avoid direct eye contact with her persuasive friend. This would not be easy.

"But you *always* spend Christmas with us. Ever since your parents ran off to Africa without you." Gillian's fair brows arched. "Or are they coming home this year?"

"No, they're not coming home."

"I just don't get them." Gillian blew on her mocha. "I mean, it's nice they want to help poor people over there and everything, but to leave their only child and just —"

"We've been down this road before." Emma stifled irritation. "You know that I love how my parents run the mission school in Uganda. It was their lifelong dream. And in their defense, they didn't even pursue it until I graduated."

"That is exactly why you need to spend Christmas with us. You're part of our family, Em." Gillian smiled smugly. "I'm not supposed to say so, but Grant told Mom that he's thinking about settling down."

"Oh, that's nice. Does your brother have a girlfriend now?"

"No, silly. Grant has always had a thing for you, Emma. You know that."

Emma resisted the urge to roll her eyes like one of her adolescent students. Grant was just one more reason to forgo another Christmas with the Landerses. But how to let Gillian down gently? "Well, I just don't think I can do —"

"You still haven't let me explain everything." Gillian held up a stop-sign hand. "What you don't know is that Dad came up with this awesome plan. We are doing a house swap for Christmas."

"A house swap?"

"Yes. You know how Dad grew up in Michigan. You've heard him get all nostalgic, whining about how he misses those white Christmases."

"A white Christmas?" Emma felt her interest pique.

"Yes. So, anyway, Dad arranged a house swap with these people in Breckenridge, Colorado. Apparently it's this awesome ski area. Not that I'm all that interested in winter sports. But Grant invited a friend to come." Her pale blue eyes twinkled. "Remember that dreamy Harris from last Christmas?"

Emma nodded. Mostly she remembered Gillian's obsession with a guy who barely noticed Gil was breathing . . . and then how he left early and an argument erupted between Gillian and her brother as a result.

"It seems that Harris is really into skiing, so he's totally down with this Colorado trip. Won't it be fun, Em?"

The image of Christmas with snow was truly appealing. Emma had never seen real snow before. Not in person anyway. Still . . . she wasn't so sure about a destination holiday with the Landerses. So many things could go wrong, and home would be more than a short drive away.

"So, here's the deal. I *have* to take you with us. It'll balance things out. You can occupy Grant while I occupy his handsome

10

friend." Gillian giggled.

Emma knew Gillian well enough not to be surprised or even insulted by the implication. She was used to being taken for granted by Gillian — it was just Gil's way. But their friendship had deep roots . . . old ties that Emma couldn't ignore. But another Christmas with the Landerses? "I don't know, Gillian. I was sort of planning on using winter break to work on my music. I've been working on some new songs and —"

"Did you have a special gig or something?"

"No, nothing special, or even for certain. But besides getting a lot of practice time on my guitar, I'm lined up to perform at McCreary's Pub. They didn't give me the date yet but promised me something during the holidays."

"Oh, you play for McCreary's all the time. That's no big deal."

Emma resisted the urge to point out that it was a big deal. At least to her.

"Think about it, Em. A paid ski vacation in Breckenridge, Colorado — and spending Christmas with me and my family. Seriously, how can you turn that down?"

"A white Christmas does sound cool." Emma felt her reserve melting.

"And I almost forgot — Dad already reserved your airline ticket — we're all going first class so you've got to come with us. Everyone will be devastated if you don't. You're like part of the family. Please, say you will. Consider it your Christmas present to me this year. *Please!*"

Emma softened. "Okay, Gil, you talked me into it."

"The clock is ticking, girlfriend." Gillian set down her coffee mug. "Time to go shopping for some chic winter garb. I hear it's cold up there. And you and I are going to look like a million bucks."

Emma knew it was pointless to resist Gil's plan to shop until she dropped — Emma, not Gillian — especially since she'd already agreed to spend the day with her friend. Now Gil's BMW was pointed westward, with Gil's favorite singer, Gunner Price, blasting through the sound system. Although Phoenix was considered the shopping mecca of the Southwest, it didn't seem ideal for finding appropriate winter clothes. But this was Gillian — and shopping wasn't just her hobby, it was her passion. So Emma wasn't too surprised when Gillian found a ski store with all sorts of winter-friendly apparel.

"Not that one," Gillian told Emma with a frown.

Emma checked out the dark olive-green

parka in the full-length mirror. "I like it." She zipped it up. "It feels snug and warm. Plus it's been marked down."

"For good reason. It's dull and drab."

"I like dull and drab." Emma pulled her long ponytail out of the collar, turning to check out the back of the coat in the mirror. She liked that it was cut long — it would keep her backside warm and offer some padding if she fell down during a ski lesson, which seemed inevitable.

"But with your striking black hair and dark eyes, you should be wearing something more colorful." Gillian held up a bright turquoise coat. "Like this."

"No thanks. That is so not me."

"Good point. My parka is blue — like my eyes. You need something different. How about this one?" She held up a hot pink jacket with a lot of silver snaps and zippers.

"Thanks, but no thanks."

"But you'd look like an Asian princess in it."

Emma laughed. "Will you ever get over that, Gil? My grandmother might've been Japanese, but she certainly wasn't royalty."

"Yeah, yeah. I know she was a starving war bride. But you don't know, she could've been a descendant of some emperor or something. I mean, you've always had kind

13

of a regal look."

"In your imagination." Emma took off the green parka. "I think I'll take this one." She looked at Gillian. "That powder blue looks great on you, Gil. It's almost the same shade as your eyes."

"That's what I thought too. Plus it shows off my tan."

"You'll be the cutest ski bunny up there," Emma teased.

"Are you suggesting I'm a poser?" Gillian struck a pose then laughed.

Emma tried on a knit hat. "So you really don't plan to give it a try?"

"Are you kidding? I don't want to make a fool of myself. Not in front of Harris. I'll be waiting at the lodge with my hot cocoa when you guys come down. Hopefully they won't be bringing you down on a stretcher."

"Thanks for that vote of confidence."

"I'm kidding. We know you're the athletic one. I just wish you wanted to be a snow bunny with me. We go so good together, Em. Our looks totally complement each other."

Emma's smile felt placating. How many times had she heard that before? Early on in their friendship, she'd worried that Gillian considered her a fashion accessory. But over time, she'd figured out that Gillian was just Gillian. Slightly shallow, yes, but sincere and fun-loving too. And if anyone ever tried to take advantage of Emma, Gillian was always the first one to her rescue. How could Emma not remain loyal to her?

TWO

West Prescott never would've agreed to a holiday house swap if his mother hadn't pressured him into it. And just less than two weeks ago. Most guys in their late thirties didn't let their parents push them around, but West's relationship with his mom was special. Now to discover it was actually his stepfather behind this last-minute deal — well, that changed things.

"So, you're telling me that Drew dreamed up this half-baked plan?" West asked his sister as he shoved summery clothes into a duffel bag.

"Yes, but I think it'll be fun," McKenzie said on her end of the phone. "And you should see the house, West. Didn't Mom send you photos? It's fabulous."

"I'll admit the place looks pretty swanky. But palm trees and eighty degrees don't sound much like Christmas to me." He zipped the duffel.

"Spoken like a true songwriter," she teased.

"A songwriter who wants to spend Christmas in his own home." West went out to the catwalk, tossing his duffel bag down to the first floor. He gazed longingly at the wide-open living room, the tall stone fireplace, the comfortable furnishings. "And it's all decorated for Christmas here too."

"You're kidding! You decorated for us?"

"Well, not me personally. I let Gunner Price use my house for his Christmas video six weeks ago. Professional decorators came in and really did a number on my place. You should see it." He gazed down at the enormous tree, decked out in mountain style with little cabins, miniature moose, snowshoes, and pine cones. He'd liked it so much, he'd actually purchased it — and everything else — from the designer. "We've literally decked the halls." He described the garlands and lights. "And all these old-fashioned lanterns that look like the real thing but use batteries instead of flames."

"I don't know which is more impressive," McKenzie said. "That Gunner Price was just there or that your house is already decorated for Christmas."

"I know. This house has never looked more Christmassy."

"Why didn't you mention it earlier?"

"Because I'd hoped to surprise you guys at Christmas."

"Bummer. Now I feel bad, West. I'm sorry we won't be there to see it."

"Yeah, yeah, well, those Arizona house swappers will probably appreciate it." West grabbed his backpack on the landing then hurried down the massive wooden staircase. He would've slid on the handrail, but the hand-hewn logs were artistically wrapped with a realistic green garland, complete with twinkle lights and red plaid bows.

"I'm sure the house swappers will love everything there, West. It's a beautiful home. But, on the same token, my boys are gonna love that amazing pool at the Arizona house. Did you see how big it is? It has a waterfall and a hot tub and —"

"Yeah, can't wait to hit the hot tub in ninety-degree heat." West picked up his duffel bag and gave his big lodge-style house one last look. The Christmas decor was so nicely done. Even the gigantic fake tree looked like the real deal. Palm trees couldn't begin to compete. "Well, at least I can work on my tan down there in the sunny Southwest."

"Now, that's the spirit, bro. You better skedaddle if you're going to meet us at the airport on time. The traffic is something else coming up from the Springs. I'm surprised you can't hear Jeremy groaning."

"I can imagine. But I'll bet the traffic is mostly on its way *into* Colorado — not out." West punched in the security code then stepped out the enormous hand-carved front door. "And they're predicting a dump of fresh snow before Christmas Eve." He stepped back to gaze at his home. His manager had encouraged him to buy it after the songs he'd created for Gunner Price's album went platinum several years ago, and West had never regretted it. Although, as he hid the key in the designated spot, he did regret leaving it — and to strangers too.

"And while your house swappers are freezing their hind ends off on the slopes, we'll all be poolside, soaking up sun and sipping on something cool and frosty." She laughed. "It'll be rough, but I think you can handle it."

"Oh, sure, sis, as long as *you're* happy." His tone turned sarcastic as he crunched through the crusty snow. "You and dear old Drew." He felt a tinge of guilt for knocking their stepdad. Especially since McKenzie liked him.

"Oh, West. That wasn't nice." She paused at the sound of kids' voices. "Anyway, I gotta settle a dispute. The boys can't agree on the video playing in the back seat at the moment. See you in Denver."

As he unlocked his Jeep, West knew he'd have to apologize to his sister. She was probably feeling defensive of their stepdad by now. And it wasn't that West didn't like Drew. It was simply that he'd never gotten to know him very well. And now he resented how Drew had talked his mom into this whole last-minute house swap biz. West had only agreed because he thought his mom wanted it. He smacked the steering wheel and blew out an exasperated sigh. Why was he being so petty?

"Get over yourself," he said aloud. "It's Christmastime . . . and it's your family . . . and it's not worth sulking over." For Mom's sake — and McKenzie's — he needed to get it together before arriving in Denver where they'd be waiting. Otherwise he'd wind up being the Grinch spoiling everyone's Christmas. Time to straighten up and get into the Christmas spirit!

To assist with his holiday attitude adjustment, he started playing Gunner Price's Christmas album off of iTunes. And it wasn't just ego wanting to hear his own creations playing, because most of these were old Christmas classics. Only three had been written by TW Prescott — West's professional name. He had to admit they weren't bad, maybe they'd even be classics a hundred years from now. That'd be cool.

It was funny being a songwriter. Even if you were talented and successful — words that folks in the music industry used to describe West — you could still slip right under everyone's celebrity radar. And that came in pretty handy. Sometimes he'd be with Gunner and suddenly the fans were mobbing him. But West could just slip away because no one recognized him. And he liked that. At one time, when he was still young and naive and a little too full of himself, West had aspired to perform his own music in front of packed stadiums. Now he felt grateful — for the most part — to simply be the creative guy behind the scenes. Oh, he still played and sang for family and friends sometimes, but the limelight had lost its allure.

After an hour behind the wheel singing along to Christmas tunes, he was feeling pretty Christmassy — until he hit the Denver traffic. Suddenly, all good will toward men seemed to melt like the brown slush alongside the jam-packed multilane freeway. If this kept up, he might actually miss his flight. He chuckled. Maybe that would be a blessing in disguise. Except that his mom and sis would be disappointed, and he didn't want that. He needed to pick it up.

Navigating his Jeep through bumper-to-bumper traffic, West remembered the years following his dad's death — the way he and Mom and McKenzie became the three musketeers, banding together to squeak by on Mom's meager wages as a hotel manager. Their little Christmases had never been fancy, but they stood out in memory as the sweetest ones ever. And they'd always made a point to be together at Christmas. But in Arizona . . . it wouldn't be easy.

By the time he'd parked and was riding the shuttle to the terminal, West realized he'd made a huge mistake. Not in swapping his house for Christmas, although that was a doozy. But in his rush to get out of Breckenridge on time, and distracted by McKenzie's disturbing last-minute phone call, he'd left his leather case of music at home. And not in his studio — where it would be relatively safe — but right out on the dining room table. In plain sight. He'd meant to grab it before heading out — then totally forgot!

He considered the options. The housekeeper, who'd nearly been finished before he left, would be long gone by now. He could call a neighbor and ask them to go by and pick up the case and have it sent to him — except that the Arizona house-swapping family was due to arrive this afternoon. For all he knew, they could be there by now. He wasn't exactly worried they would snoop in his private things, most of which he'd stashed in a locked closet, but he needed those music sheets with him.

He had several songs in development right now. Ones that he'd promised to finish and deliver shortly after Christmas. His manager's warning to quit putting songs down on paper but trust a computer instead rang through his mind. But West liked doing it the old-fashioned way.

As he hopped off the shuttle, he dug out his phone, hitting speed dial for Mom. "Where are you?" she asked with concern. "You should be here by now, West."

"I am here," he said quickly.

"Good. Then hurry to the gate. McKenzie and Jeremy and the boys just got here. And it looks like they're getting ready to announce board —"

"I'm not even through security, Mom, but —"

"What on earth? How can you —"

"I got stuck in traffic, but it's worse than

that." He quickly explained his dilemma. "I've got to go home and get my music. You know how important that is."

"Yes, of course. You must get it." She sounded disappointed.

"You guys go ahead and board your flight. I'll catch a red-eye tonight. Or tomorrow if they're booked. Or I'll fly standby. Or something."

"Oh, West, you've got to make it down there." She lowered her voice. "It's already disappointing not to be spending Christmas at your house in Breckenridge. McKenzie just told me about how you got it all decorated so nicely. But if you're not in Arizona with us — well, it just won't be Christmas."

"I know, Mom. I'll get down there somehow. Planes, trains, or automobiles." He tried to sound nonchalant as he got back in line for the shuttle. "I might not be thrilled about Christmas with no snow, but I'll do whatever it takes to be with you and McKenzie and everyone. I'll be there."

"I know you will. Just let me know your plans and when you'll arrive."

He boarded the shuttle and promised to keep her informed. As the bus chugged back to the parking lots, West got on his phone to set up a new flight and was immediately put on hold. The music was obnoxious, but

24

he slipped in his earbud just the same. He would leave it on hold for as long as it took. Setting his personal feelings aside, he knew that somehow he had to make it down to Arizona for Christmas.

THREE

Emma couldn't believe it. The trip had
barely begun, and everything seemed to be
going sideways. It started before they even
boarded the plane. Mr. Landers was upset
to discover a problem with the tickets.
Although they'd gotten through security
without a hitch, it came to their attention as
they were boarding that only the Landerses'
tickets were for first class. Their guests,
Emma and Harris, had been assigned to
coach.

As Mr. Landers tried to sort it out on the
phone with his assistant, Mrs. Landers
argued with the woman at the gate, insist-
ing they'd paid for six first-class tickets.
"And that is what we want."

"I'm happy to sit in coach," Emma eagerly
told them, hoping to smooth this thing over
before it grew worse. "It's a short flight. I
don't mind a bit."

"But we booked first class," Mrs. Landers

insisted.

"The flight is booked full," the woman firmly told her. "There are no available seats in first class. If you want to surrender any of your tickets, we have people waiting for standby, and it's time for first class to start boarding."

"No, we're good." Mr. Landers pocketed his phone. "My assistant just clarified that she could only secure four first-class seats and the other two are coach."

"Coach works for me." Emma nodded at the woman.

"Me too," Harris chimed in.

Mr. Landers handed over the boarding passes with an apology. "Thanks for understanding."

"Thanks for bringing us with you," Emma said brightly. "Do you know this will be my first time to see real snow?"

"No kidding?" He grinned. "Well, you're going to love it, Emma."

"Well, I won't love it." Mrs. Landers frowned at her husband. "And I don't like how this is starting out, Gary. It's like a bad omen."

"Don't be ridiculous, Lisa. It was just a little hiccup. And you heard them, Emma and Harris don't mind flying coach."

"Well, I mind." She glanced around with

27

a nervous expression. "I get the strongest feeling we should've stayed home for Christmas."

"It's going to be just fine," Mr. Landers declared. "And look, it's time for us to board."

"Where are the kids?" Mrs. Landers looked around anxiously.

"Gillian's getting a magazine," Emma told her.

"And Grant's using the little boys' room," Harris said.

Just as the older Landerses got in line, Gillian and Grant returned, getting in line behind them. Meanwhile, Emma and Harris waited.

"Come on," Gillian called out to them.

"Not yet," Emma said, realizing that Gillian probably didn't know about the tickets yet. "We'll see you soon." She waved as Mr. Landers ushered his family through the line.

"Are you bummed about not flying first class?" Harris asked her.

"Not at all." She smiled. "I'm just glad I get to go."

"Is that true what you said — about never having seen snow?"

She nodded self-consciously.

"Seriously?"

"Seriously. My family's not wealthy like

28

Gillian's. When we went on a vacation, it was always in a car, and never much beyond the Southwest. Although I have been to Florida to visit my grandmother."

"So you obviously don't know how to ski."

"Obviously."

"Do you think you'd like to learn?"

"I'd love to learn."

"Are you athletic at all?" He studied her.

"I like to think so." She told him about the sports she'd played in school. "And I work out three times a week."

"You'll be fine then." He grinned. "I'm a good teacher."

"Looks like our turn to board," she said as their section was announced. Before long they were stowing carry-on bags and getting their seats. Hers was by the window and his was next to her. "This isn't so bad." She fastened her seat belt.

"Easy for you to say. *I* got the middle seat."

"Want to trade?"

"No." He shrugged. "I'll be okay."

Emma cringed as a woman and a wailing baby took the seat on the other side of Harris. "Sure you don't want to trade seats?" she whispered.

He chuckled. "Thanks, but like you said, it's not a long flight." He moved a bit closer to her to make room for the woman struggling with her fussing baby and carry-on bag.

Emma gazed out the window, noticing the heat waves blurring the tarmac's surface. "Looks like it's warming up out there," she said loudly enough to be heard over the crying infant.

"Might get up to eighty this week. Could break a record." Harris turned to face her — or to escape the loud scene next to him.

"That makes me even happier to get to a cooler climate for Christmas."

"You don't like warm weather?"

"I don't know. I guess I've never given it much thought. I mean, it's all I've known. I was born in Tempe and I still live there."

"Then you must be happy there."

She shrugged. "Or just stuck."

"Why stuck?"

As the plane taxied out in preparation for takeoff, she explained about her parents teaching in Uganda. "They let me live in their house. It's just a little house, but they want to come back to it when they're done. Like I said, my family is nothing like the Landers family. But I get to live rent free. And that means I don't have to teach full time."

"So you're a teacher?"

She explained about getting on the substi-

30

tute teachers' list in her district. "Mostly high school. Middle school sometimes, but I try to avoid that if I can. It gets pretty grueling."

"Then why do it? Teaching, I mean."

She laughed. "To pay the bills. Only working part time gives me the chance to pursue my real passion."

"What's that?" His dark brows arched.

"Music."

"Ah, you're a musician."

"Yeah, I like to think so." She told him a bit about playing guitar and occasionally performing in local venues.

"So you must be pretty good."

"I wouldn't say that." She grinned. "But you can."

The flight attendant was going through the safety routine, and Emma pretended to read the instructions, but Harris just chuckled. "Do you have a flying phobia?" he whispered. "Need to hold my hand?"

Emma laughed. "No thanks, I'm fine."

After takeoff, he asked her about Gillian. "How did you two become friends? No offense, but I don't think I've ever known two friends who were more complete opposites." His eyes twinkled. "Actually, I think that might be a compliment — *to you.*"

"Oh." A light bulb went on. Harris was

signaling her that he had no interest in Gillian. And was he flirting with her? This wouldn't be good. "Well, there's more to Gillian than meets the eye," she said carefully.

"Uh-huh?" He nodded thoughtfully. "She's not bad-looking, in that blonde, slave-to-fashion way. But I like your style better, Emma. Much more easygoing. Like you're comfortable in your own skin." He unzipped his jacket. "And you're genuinely nice."

"Uh, thanks. But Gillian is nice too." She measured her words. "I know she comes across as, well, demanding at times. But she was sort of raised like that. High expectations, you know?"

"Sounds like you're trying to paint her with a gentle brush."

"No, I'm just trying to help you understand her." She told him the story of how Gillian had come to Emma's rescue in college. "I just couldn't seem to find my way. Not directionally. But I'd sort of known who I was in high school. I fit in. So college made me feel lost. Gillian reached out to me and, although I was living at home, she invited me to join her sorority."

"Oh . . . sorority sisters, I get it."

"Not exactly. I mean, I did join, and it

helped me to make some friends. But one night there was a party there, and, well, it got a little out of hand. I suppose I was in over my head. This guy was — well, you can probably guess — not so nice. And guess who came to my rescue?"

"Gillian?"

"Yes. She was like a mother bear. I suppose it sounds like I'm exaggerating, but it honestly felt like she saved my life at the time. I was still upset, and I didn't want to go home. My parents are rather conservative and extremely overprotective. I knew they wouldn't understand. But I didn't want to stay in the sorority house either, so Gillian took me home with her. She drove us up to Scottsdale, and we stayed there all weekend, and I guess that's when we first became friends."

"Were you blown away with how wealthy her family is?"

"Yeah, I guess so. At first. But it's been about fourteen years now. I've gotten used to it."

"You and Gillian are still close friends?"

"Well, not as close as it might seem. I really don't see that much of her. On holidays and things. But we live in different worlds."

"Speaking of Gillian, here comes her

brother."

"Oh?" Emma looked up to see Grant maneuvering down the aisle toward them.

"You guys having fun slumming?" he teased.

"No complaints," Emma shot back.

"Gillian suggested I come back and offer to switch seats. I guess she's under the impression I'm a gentleman." He laughed. "How about it?"

"I'm okay," Emma said.

"I didn't mean you, Emma." Grant pointed to Harris. "You want to go sit in first class?"

"I'm fine," Harris said a bit sharply.

Grant looked surprised, but before he could question this, the flight attendant asked him to move back to his seat so she could get the beverage cart through.

"Interesting," Harris said. "Didn't seem very gentlemanly to me."

Emma didn't know what to say. Gillian had obviously hoped to sit with Harris — in first class — until Denver. How would she react to discover he'd declined her brother's generous offer?

"I guess that might be like the writing on the wall." Harris put down his food tray. "Gillian wants her way . . . but I plan to stay put."

Emma just nodded, wondering how she could smooth this over with Gillian later. "Uh-oh," she whispered.

"Huh?" He looked at her.

"Here comes Gillian now." Emma forced a smile for her friend.

"Hey, you two. My parents feel bad you got stuck back here in baggage."

"It's not exactly baggage," Harris said lightly.

"Are you sure?" she asked him. "Looks pretty tight to me. Anyway, since Harris didn't want to come up to first class to stretch his legs, well, I think you should go, Emma."

"I appreciate the offer, but I'm okay."

"My parents feel like it's only fair," Gillian insisted. "I promised you first class, Emma." She placed a hand on the mom's shoulder. "You don't mind getting up for my friend, do you?" She smiled brightly.

"I guess not." The woman struggled to unbuckle her seat belt, then forced her baby onto Gillian. "With a little help."

"What?" Gillian's eyes grew wide.

As the baby cried, Harris looked helplessly at Emma.

"You better hurry, Harris." Gillian shoved the baby back toward the waiting mother. "Let Emma out before the beverage cart comes back. Come on, Emma, you're moving on up, girlfriend."

Not knowing a graceful way out of this, Emma tugged her purse from under the seat and followed Harris out to the aisle so that Gillian could take the window seat. The baby continued to cry, and the displaced mom looked very irritated. Even laid-back Harris seemed perplexed as he slid back into the middle seat. But Gillian appeared obliviously pleased with her new seating arrangement. Emma gave them all a little wave, then hurried up to first class, where — no surprise — Grant had an empty seat and a wide smile waiting for her.

"Welcome to leg room," he said.

"Thanks." She sat. "It is better up here."

"Worth the effort, don't you think?"

"I just hope Gillian doesn't mind how cramped it is back there."

"Oh, Gil won't mind." His eyes twinkled like he was in on the joke. "And I just ordered you a champagne. It's complimentary, you know. So when the attendant sets it down, don't be surprised if it tells you how pretty you look."

"Huh?" Emma blinked.

"It's *complimentary.*" He chuckled. "Get it?"

"Oh, yeah." She couldn't control herself

from rolling her eyes this time. "It's been a while, Grant. I guess I totally forgot your sense of humor."

"Great. I'll entertain you some more."

For the next hour and a half, she listened to Grant either telling lame jokes or more about investment finances than she ever wanted to know. At least the seat was comfy. Better yet, Gillian was happy — Emma hoped. And, really, Emma felt relieved to be away from Harris. Certainly, he was nice enough. But just a bit too interested in her. And that would not make for a happy holiday with Gillian. Besides that, Harris wasn't Emma's type. She wasn't sure why that was exactly, but she felt pretty certain of it. Still, it had been entertaining to visit with him — better than being talked to death by Grant. Hopefully this wasn't a forecast of the upcoming week. At least there would be snow.

FOUR

Emma wasn't surprised that she got stuck in the back seat with Grant on the trip from Denver to Breckenridge. Harris had exchanged glances with her when Gillian assigned the seating order. He'd seemed even more troubled than Emma. But then he hadn't thought to put his bags between him and Gil. Emma had taken care of that by wedging her bags between her and Grant.

Because, even though it was a large and luxurious SUV, everyone was packed in between carry-on bags and coats, with the larger bags in back and some gear stashed in the cargo carrier on top. Mrs. Landers had already lodged her complaints about only having one rental vehicle for this trip, but Mr. Landers had assured her there would be another car available at the Breckenridge house. "And it's only ninety minutes."

"Ninety minutes of being stuffed in here

like sardines?" she'd retorted, which naturally led to some bickering in the front seat.

Emma blocked it out by focusing on the view out the window. "It's so beautiful," she declared. "I can't believe it."

"What is *so beautiful*?" Mrs. Landers asked sharply.

"The snow." Emma gazed with wonder at the white mountains.

"Snow?" Mrs. Landers laughed, but not with humor. "It looks more like brown slush to me. Honestly, Gary, I thought Colorado would be much prettier than this."

"Give it a chance," he told her. "We're barely out of Denver."

"And I don't mean the snow along the freeway," Emma clarified. "I meant the snow up there on the mountains. Isn't it pristine? I can't believe I'm actually looking at snowy mountains. I already feel Christmassy."

"According to my weather app, they're expecting more snow by tonight," Harris said. "Should be perfect for skiing."

"I just hope we don't get more snow before we get there." Mrs. Landers sounded anxious. "I've heard this drive can be treacherous in snow. Especially for people who aren't used to driving in these conditions. People like us."

"Don't worry, Lisa," Mr. Landers reassured her. "You know, I grew up in Michigan. I can drive in snow. And this Escalade has four-wheel drive. We'll be perfectly fine."

"And if we do get stranded in a blizzard, I've still got a lot of munchies in my bag — and I'll happily auction them off to you guys," Grant teased.

"I still don't know why we did this silly house swap." Mrs. Landers's tone grew more irritated. "Leaving our lovely home to risk our lives up here in the desolate mountains. It's perfectly ridiculous. We don't even ski."

"Speak for yourself."

"You're telling me you know how to ski?" she asked.

"I used to ski — as a kid. Admittedly, it's been a while, but hopefully it's like riding a bike. What do you think, Harris? You're the expert here."

"I think a few lessons and you'll be tearing up the mountain."

Mr. Landers laughed. "As long as the mountain doesn't tear me up."

"Oh, Gary, you can't be serious. Skiing at your age? You'll probably break your neck, and I'll have to spend my holidays taking care of you."

"If I break my neck, I'll be in the hospital."

40

"Okay, then your leg."

"No one is going to break anything, Lisa." His tone matched hers in aggravation. "Good grief. Just relax and enjoy this!"

"Yeah, Mom," Gillian chimed in. "Take a chill pill."

"Thank you, but I can do without your sarcasm, Gillian. If I remember correctly, you were not in favor of this trip at first either, not until you found out —"

"Oh, Mom, don't be such a spoilsport," Gillian interrupted. "It's Christmastime. We're supposed to have fun, remember?"

"That's right," Mr. Landers agreed. "Listen to your daughter's wisdom."

And just like that the first family feud of the trip erupted. Gillian and her mom going at it. Grant stepping in to defend his mother by reprimanding his sister. Mr. Landers telling everyone to shut up so he could focus on driving. And Harris laughing loudly as if the whole thing were highly amusing. Meanwhile, Emma kept her eyes on the passing scenery, which seemed to get more and more beautiful. She was tempted to comment on it, except she felt her appreciation for Colorado's mountains and snow had incited the whole squabble in the first place.

"I feel like we're driving through a sweet

41

old-fashioned Christmas movie," she said quietly to Grant. "The snow up here is so pretty. Much better than it looked in Denver."

He looked out his window, then nodded. "I have to admit, it is nice."

Harris turned around in his seat to face the two of them. "Wait until you see Breckenridge. It's even better."

"Are we there yet, Dad?" Grant yelled out in a teasing tone.

"Very funny. I just hope we get there before dark."

"According to that last sign and my phone, we should be there a half hour before sunset," Harris told him. "We're only about twenty minutes from Breckenridge right now."

"Thanks, Harris. I should make you my navigator," Mr. Landers said.

"Look!" Mrs. Landers cried out in a panicky tone.

"What is it?" Mr. Landers demanded.

"Snow."

"Of course it's snow," he growled back at her. "We're in Colorado."

"I mean snowflakes are falling — *from the sky.* What if it turns into a blizzard?"

"What if there's an earthquake and mountains fall down on us?" Gillian teased. "Seriously, Mom, you need to just chill out."

And now the family feud started all over again. But fortunately, the snowflakes didn't turn into a blizzard and the mountains didn't tumble down. Before long, they were driving through the most picturesque town Emma had ever seen. "Wow," she said quietly, "this is really, really beautiful."

"Yeah, not bad," Grant said. And the others began to comment favorably as well, except for Mrs. Landers. Her arms folded tightly in front of her, she stared straight forward, not saying a word. She was clearly in a bad mood, but hopefully that would change once they got settled in.

"Well, here we are," Mr. Landers announced as he pulled up in front of the house.

"Is this it?" Mrs. Landers sounded unimpressed. "I thought it would be bigger."

"Me too," Gillian agreed.

"It's got five bedrooms and six baths." Mr. Landers turned off the engine.

"It doesn't look that big from here," Mrs. Landers said. "Are you sure this is the right place, Gary?"

"According to the address."

"Why is that Jeep parked in front?" she demanded.

"Probably for our use. First dibs," Grant

said. "Looks like a nice one too."

Mr. Landers opened the door. "Come on, everyone. This is definitely the right place. You boys start unloading the car while I open things up."

"I think it's absolutely picture perfect." As she got out, Emma took in the wood and rock structure. It was rustically handsome — and beautifully dusted in white snow. She scooped up a handful of snow, holding it close to her face and sniffing.

"Snow has no smell," Gillian teased. "But maybe you should taste it."

"Okay, I will." Emma took a nibble and Gillian laughed.

"Oh, Emma — I can't believe you. I hope it doesn't make you sick."

"How could anything so fresh and clean make me sick?"

"Come on, ladies," Mr. Landers called out as he opened the door. "I need to punch in the security code."

Eager to see more, Emma hurried inside, taking it all in. The foyer floor was slate, and the staircase was made of logs. The furnishings were rustic but beautiful, and everything — from antler lamps to Native American rugs — seemed to fit together impeccably. To top it all off, it was beautifully decorated for Christmas. The garlands on the banisters looked so real, she had to touch them. And the enormous tree with all its charming woodsy decorations not only looked real, it smelled real too. Had someone sprayed it with pine scent? "Oh, my goodness," she gushed. "It's all absolutely perfect."

"Perfect?" Mrs. Landers was not impressed. "It reminds me of that old John Candy movie — *The Great Outdoors* — where they stayed in that wretched cabin and —"

"I love that movie," Emma told her. "And the cabin was great after they cleaned it up. But this one's spotlessly clean." She pointed to the tall Christmas tree by the fireplace. "Did you see those snowshoe and ski ornaments? And those tiny cabins with little lights inside? Doesn't it all make you feel Christmassy?"

"If you ask me the decorations are all wrong," Mrs. Landers declared.

"Wrong?" Mr. Landers demanded. "How can they be wrong?"

"Oh, they're fine if you like things like pine cones and moose antlers and all that rustic sort of nonsense. Personally, I'd rather see some glitz and glamour — sparkle and shine. Like at our house."

"But this is a rustic house," he argued.

45

"Just look around and —"

"All I want to look at right now is the master suite. And it better be on the ground floor." She turned to her husband. "Do you happen to know where it's located, Gary? Or must I go exploring this caveman house?"

"Caveman house?" Emma couldn't help herself.

"Yes. That's what it reminds me of. I expect to see Fred Flintstone coming around the corner any minute." Mrs. Landers laughed.

"The Flintstone house was short and squat," Gillian pointed out. "This one is tall."

"Fine, it's a tall caveman house. I prefer a single-level house." She frowned at Mr. Landers. "Have you figured it out yet?"

He held up the paperwork, which appeared to include a floor plan. "Looks like the master suite is up on top."

"On top?" She glared at him. "On top of what? Old Smokey?"

"On the third floor," he said cautiously.

"You've got to be kidding. Does this place have an elevator?"

"No, no, I don't think so."

"You expect me to go up and down *three* flights of stairs with my sore knee?"

"Actually, it would only be two flights, Lisa."

"Gary!"

He pointed to the paper. "According to this, there's one bedroom on the first floor, and it looks like it has its own bath. We'll just use that one." He gave her directions, and after she left, he turned to Emma and Gillian. "And which bedrooms would you ladies like?"

"I don't want the third floor either," Gillian announced. "The only place I do stairs is at my fitness club."

"Well, there are three bedrooms on the second floor. Take one of those."

"I don't mind a third-floor bedroom," Emma told him. "Unless someone else wants it."

"It's all yours, Emma. That leaves the other two second-floor bedrooms for the guys. Sure you won't mind being up there by yourself?"

"Not at all." She paused at the foot of the stairs, trying to think of a way to encourage Gillian's dad. The old guy was trying so hard . . . and no one seemed to appreciate it. "The third floor sounds heavenly to me. In fact, this whole house is just wonderful. I absolutely love it."

"Listen to our little Pollyanna," Gillian

teased. "Which is probably why you always get invited back."

"Thanks." Emma made a face at her. "And thank you, Mr. Landers. I really do appreciate it. This house seems like the most perfect place to spend Christmas."

"Well, I'm glad someone is happy." Mr. Landers's smile seemed grateful.

"I doubt the guys will mind you getting the third-floor room," Gillian told Emma. "But I'm going to snag the best second-floor room before they come in."

"I might have to bunk with one of the guys." Mr. Landers chuckled. "If Lisa doesn't get into a better mood."

As Emma scaled the beautiful staircase, slowly going up two flights, she wasn't so sure he was kidding. The way Gillian's parents interacted was so different than her own parents. They rarely disagreed on anything. At least Mr. and Mrs. Landers cooled off quickly. Still, she longed for a relationship more like her parents'. If she ever found that special someone . . . some-day . . . she hoped they wouldn't waste a lot of precious time bickering.

FIVE

West couldn't believe he'd gotten trapped in his own home like this, but when that family suddenly burst in on him, he had just ducked into the kitchen to gather some food and drinks to take with him on his drive back to Denver. He'd already rescued his music, but realizing that snow was forecasted, which could mean a highway delay, he knew provisions were advisable. Even if he made it to Denver with no problem, he could be stuck there all night if he didn't secure that standby seat. Airport food had its limitations, so taking his own just made sense. What didn't make sense was that he'd allowed this unappreciative Arizona family to take over his home. Already, he didn't like them.

Hiding out in the walk-in pantry, he'd overheard enough of their conversation to realize that one woman in particular — she sounded like the mom — was not the least

49

bit happy to be here. She'd complained about everything from the location of the master suite to the Christmas decorations. What kind of woman complains about Christmas decorations? He stuffed a handful of energy bars into his backpack then, not hearing more voices, he peeked out to see if the coast was clear.

Convinced they were all settling into their rooms, West slipped out the back unnoticed. But when he got to the driveway, he realized his Jeep was blocked in by an oversized SUV. Looking up, he saw the sky was getting dark, and not just with dusky twilight. The clouds were heavy and gray. That snowstorm was coming earlier than predicted. He would be a fool to try to make it back to Denver in a blizzard. Besides that, his Jeep was blocked in.

He pulled out his phone. By now his family should have made it to Arizona. "Hey, Mom," he said lightly after getting redirected to her voice mail. "Looks like I'll be waylaid here for the night." He explained the weather, promising to get out on the next available flight tomorrow, then hung up.

For a moment, he felt relieved at the thought of sleeping in his own bed tonight — and then he remembered his house had been taken over by aliens. *Aliens from Arizona.* Maybe he could write a humorous song about that. In the meantime, he'd have to sleep in his studio tonight. Fortunately, it was separate from the house and had a fairly comfortable Murphy bed — and it was not included in this stupid house swap. He did agree with *Mrs. I-Hate-Everything* on one thing — trading homes at Christmastime was completely ridiculous. Never again!

As he unlocked his studio, he considered unloading his Jeep, but then he'd just have to reload it again in the morning. Besides, he had a few necessities in the studio to get him by. He hadn't felt the need for a studio when he'd purchased this house several years ago, but the property had been priced right and his manager had suggested West use it for a caretaker's cottage. Instead, West had used it for himself and his music. And if he had company — like his family who always came for holidays — it was a great getaway. Because as much as he loved his three energetic nephews, he didn't appreciate that they treated his musical instruments like toys. Still, he'd have been much happier if it were his family settling into the house — instead of those aliens from Arizona.

Although one of the aliens had sounded okay. Based on what he'd overheard, she wasn't a member of the family, which might explain why she sounded nicer. Her name was Emma . . . and she seemed to like his house. In fact, he'd felt relieved to hear she was the one who'd occupy his bedroom. Hopefully, she wouldn't mind the dead bolt on his walk-in closet door. He'd had it installed after his mother announced the house-swapping plan. Then he'd stashed all his personal items in there and locked it. There were empty drawers in the bureau that this Emma person could use. He wondered what she looked like. He'd liked the sound of her voice, but for all he knew, she could be fifty years old and built like a linebacker. Still, he didn't think so.

Not liking the idea of leaving his music in the Jeep all night, West decided to slip out there and retrieve it. Maybe he'd even work on the desert springs song tonight. Gunner had been nagging him to finish that one. West was just opening the back of his Jeep when the sound of footsteps crunching in the snow came from behind him. Startled, he turned to see a blonde woman approaching.

"What are you doing with that Jeep?" she asked with narrowed eyes.

He blinked, trying to think of an answer that wouldn't give away his identity. For some reason, he didn't want to reveal — to any of the Arizona aliens — that he was the owner of the house they were using. He didn't want to experience their judgment or listen to their complaints or be expected to provide anything other than what they were getting. He just wanted to get out of here as soon as possible without any actual interaction.

"I'm just getting something." He slammed the back of the Jeep closed before she could see his luggage inside then tucked the leather case beneath his arm, studying her with curiosity. Was this how Arizona people dressed? She wore a fur-trimmed pale blue jacket that looked brand new and not much good for skiing.

"Getting something or *stealing* something?" she demanded.

"I'm *getting* something." He held up the leather case. "This happens to belong to me — thank you very much."

"And does that Jeep belong to you too? Because I understand it belongs with the house."

"Well, yes, it does belong with the house." He tried to think of a way out of this. "But as it turns out, I'm the caretaker of the house. So I have use of the Jeep." There, that should put an end to this inquisition.

"Really? How do I know you're telling the truth? You could be a thief." She nodded to the fancy SUV. "Maybe you were going to break into that next. Looks like I came out just in time to rescue my purse." She unlocked a door, reached inside, then slamming the door, she locked it again.

"I'm not planning to steal anything from your car, but could someone move it out of the way? It's got the Jeep blocked in." He locked eyes with her.

"Oh?" She seemed to consider this. "So, seriously, *you're* the caretaker?"

"At your service." He mocked a little bow then jerked a thumb toward his studio. "And *that* is the caretaker's cottage."

"And *that* is the snow shovel." She pointed to the shovel he'd left by the front door for his guests to utilize, holding her head high like she was royalty. Maybe the Ice Princess. "Feel free to help yourself to it anytime you like."

"Seriously?" She scowled. "You're the caretaker and you expect me to shovel the snow for you?"

"Hey, it's great exercise. Very aerobic. Now if you'll excuse me, I have some other caretaking business to attend to." He knew he'd offended her, but at the moment, he didn't care. That woman was obnoxious.

Shoveling snow would probably do her some good.

"I assume you'll remove the snow," the Ice Princess called out.

"You know what they say about that assume word," he called back. As he strolled to his studio, he could feel her staring, and he imagined her snatching up the snow shovel and bopping him on the head with it. But he made it safely inside. He peeked through the blinds, hoping she'd take his hint and move that SUV. Instead, she stomped into the house. The Ice Princess was a real piece of work!

Initially, he'd thought the woman might've been Emma, but he could tell by the tone of her voice, it was the other one. He assumed she was the daughter of the cantankerous mother and the dude who'd made the arrangements for this stupid house swap.

West didn't want to know one more thing about these people. He just wanted out of here. Then he'd bide his time in Arizona until this whole crazy trade was over and done with.

SIX

Emma felt like she'd won the lottery when she saw the third-floor bedroom. It resembled the first floor with wood-plank floors, Native American rugs, beautiful western art, and rustic decor touches. The huge bed, crafted from gleaming beautiful logs and topped with a gorgeous quilt in shades of burgundy, green, and gold, was very inviting. Plus the spacious bathroom with its roomy shower, all those shower heads, and a deep freestanding tub. But it was all the windows — and the view of the mountains — that took her breath away. Everything up here was absolutely perfect — and going up two flights of stairs was a small price to pay for this kind of solitude and beauty. But hearing raised voices downstairs reminded her that she was not alone . . . and a guest.

As Emma went down the stairs, she could hear Mrs. Landers's voice, and not surprisingly, she had found something new to complain about. "What kind of place is this that they don't have toiletries in the bathroom?"

"They have the basic necessities," Mr. Landers told her.

"There's no shampoo or conditioner or shower soap or —"

"It's *not* a hotel, Lisa. Maybe you were supposed to bring those things for yourself. I brought mine. You can use them if you —"

"And smell like a man?" She scowled at him. "And the pillows on that bed. I can't sleep with a rock-hard pillow. Never mind that the bedding is substandard."

"Maybe you should complain to the caretaker." Gillian opened the refrigerator, looking around.

"Caretaker?" Mrs. Landers sounded doubtful.

"Yeah. I just met him outside."

"There's a caretaker?" he asked. "I didn't know about that."

Gil tossed him the keys. "He wants you to move the SUV, Dad. And I'll warn you, he's a total jerk."

"The listing never mentioned a caretaker. It did say that a housekeeper would be in every other day. But other than that, I thought we were on our own."

"Nope. There's a cantankerous caretaker. He's got his own cottage behind the garage. He claims that he gets to use the Jeep, which I thought you said was for us to use."

"No, I just reread the paperwork, and it seems there's a compact car in the garage that we can use. And it's equipped with a ski rack."

"Well, unless you move the SUV so the cranky caretaker can move the Jeep, we won't be able to get anything out of the garage. And we girls get first dibs on the car." Gillian winked at Emma.

"Alright, I'll go move the SUV." He reached for his jacket. "I want to make a store run anyway."

"You're not going to the store without me," Mrs. Landers told him. "In the meantime, Gillian, you go ask the caretaker about pillows and bedding. There must be something better than what's on that bed."

"Forget it, Mom. I refuse to speak to the ol' grump." Gillian shook her head. "Seriously, he's a total jerk."

"I don't care if he's Ebenezer Scrooge reincarnate. He's the caretaker, and it's his job to make the guests comfortable. Go ask him where the extra bedding is stored. I've already looked and can't find a thing."

"No way, Mom. If you want more bedding, *you* go talk to him."

"Do I have to ask you again, Gillian?" Mrs. Landers's eyes widened, and her nostrils flared.

"I need to go to the store too." Gillian flitted her eyelashes at her dad, ignoring her mom's rising anger. "I forgot a couple of things, and my bathroom doesn't have any —"

"Gillian Elizabeth!" Mrs. Landers looked like she was about to blow.

"How about if I go speak to the caretaker?" Emma quickly offered, wanting to defuse this before it got worse.

"Well, it's not fair to impose on our guest." Mrs. Landers still glared at her daughter. "But I would appreciate the help, Emma. Thank you very much. You're such a thoughtful girl. Too bad your goodness doesn't rub off on Gillian."

Hoping to escape the mother-daughter conflict that was about to escalate to a new level, Emma hurried outside. Pausing on the snow-covered path to the driveway, she allowed fat snowflakes to fall on her, even catching a couple with her tongue. Snow couldn't hurt you. She looked all around, taking in the other large homes, beautifully blanketed in snow, and the mountains behind them. This place was truly magical!

As she walked up the driveway, she spotted what looked like a caretaker's cottage and slowly approached it. Hopefully the ol' grump wasn't as bad as Gillian had described. Holding her breath, she tentatively knocked on the door, expecting a gray, grisly old man to answer. To her surprise, a younger man opened the door. Dressed in jeans and a plaid flannel shirt, he stared at her with a puzzled expression. She suddenly wondered if she'd knocked on the wrong door.

She smiled stiffly. "Sorry to bother you. I — I was looking for the caretaker, and I thought this was the right —"

"Yeah, yeah." He studied her with a furrowed brow. "This is, uh, the caretaker's cottage."

She blinked. "Oh, so . . . are *you* the caretaker?" For some reason this guy didn't look much like a caretaker to her. And she wondered why Gillian had taken such a dislike to him. Especially considering how good-looking he was — in a country boy sort of way.

He nodded with pursed lips. "And who, may I ask, are you?"

"I'm Emma. I, uh, I'm here with the Landers family. They've got the house throughout Christmas. But you probably know all about that."

"Yes, I know. And I'm West." He ran a hand through his shaggy auburn hair.

"West? That's an interesting name. I like it." Her smile was sincere now.

"Thanks." His dark green eyes flickered with interest. "So what can I do for you, Miss Emma?"

"Well, I guess we need some more linens and things. And Mrs. Landers thinks the bed pillows are a bit hard and —"

"The master suite has spare pillows and blankets in that trunk at the foot of the bed." He frowned as if she'd presented a great imposition.

"Oh, okay. Mr. and Mrs. Landers aren't using the master suite, but I can take —"

"Which room are they using?"

Emma explained how Mrs. Landers didn't want to go up the stairs. "They took the room on the first floor."

"That's good." He rubbed his chin. "So no one's using the master suite then?"

"Actually, I'm in it," she confessed. "I can't believe I scored the best room in the house. But no one seemed to mind. The view up there is so spectacular. I've never seen anything like it before. Have you ever been up there?"

He seemed amused. "Yeah, a time or two."

"Yes, of course you have. So anyway, Mrs. Landers needs some softer pillows and more bedding. Should I take things from the master suite, or is there a linen closet or something somewhere?"

He let out an irritated groan. "Yeah, yeah . . . of course."

"Maybe you can just tell me where it's located." This must be his grumpy side. "And then I can take care of it myself. I don't want to trouble you."

"Might be easier to just show you." He reached for a ski parka hanging by the door.

"Do you mind?"

The edges of his eyes crinkled like he was about to smile. "No, I don't mind." He slipped on the parka and stepped out. Then instead of going to the front door, he led her around back and, using a key, unlocked a door. "This is the mudroom." He led her through a large room that was well equipped with skis, snowboards, snowshoes, and miscellaneous other sporting goods.

"Wow, this looks like a miniature ski shop," she said. "The homeowners must be very rich."

"I guess." He shrugged as he led her through another door. "This is the laundry room." He looked around the spacious room with two sets of washers and dryers.

"There should be a cabinet in here where the linens are stored . . . somewhere."

"Meaning you don't know exactly where the linens are kept?" she asked with suspicion. Was he truly the caretaker, or was she being taken in?

"Well, this is the housekeeper's purview. Of course, she's not here right now. She only comes in three days a week — and she was just here today getting things ready for the Landers family." He tried a cabinet to reveal cleaning supplies and then another with paper products. Finally, he opened a cupboard stacked with linens and bedding. "Bingo."

"Thank you. So if we have other questions, should we direct them to you? Or wait for the housekeeper?"

He rubbed his chin. "Well, I'm not sure I'll be around during the holidays."

"Yes, of course." She nodded. "You probably have family . . . someplace to be. Naturally, you have a life."

His dark eyes twinkled. "Well, yeah. Doesn't everyone?"

She looked down at the floor. "Yes, of course."

"Are those people — the Landerses — your family?" He peered at her with a curious expression.

"No, they're not family. I'm just friends with the daughter. My parents are in Africa . . . so I spend holidays with the Landerses."

"Your parents are in Africa?"

She quickly explained about the mission school. "But that's probably too much information."

"No, I think that's really cool." He nodded. "You must be proud of them."

She nodded. "I am. Not everyone understands what they're doing . . . or why."

"So you're pretty good friends with the Landers family?" He sat on a folding counter, swinging his legs.

"I guess so. I've known Gillian for years."

"Is that the one who spoke to me in the driveway?"

"Yes. You met Gillian." She explained about Gil's brother, Grant, and his friend, Harris. "Harris is actually a good skier. So he's pretty jazzed about being up here. And I guess Grant's more of a beginner skier. But Gillian . . . not so much."

"And you?"

She laughed. "I've never skied. To be honest, I'd never even seen real snow until today."

"You're kidding!" His eyes lit up. "What do you think of it?"

64

"I love it." She sighed. "And I do want to learn to ski."

"Well, you couldn't ask for better snow."

"That's what Harris said. And he's promised to teach me."

"So are you and Harris a couple?" He slid down off the folding counter.

"No. In fact, Gillian will probably be upset if Harris gives me ski lessons."

"So they're a couple then?"

"No. Not yet. Gillian is hoping." Emma felt surprised at herself — she wasn't usually this friendly with a strange guy, and yet he was so easy to talk to . . . and so much more peaceful than Gillian and her family.

"So how will you learn to ski?"

"I thought I could sign up for a class or even private lessons. Do they have something like that up here?"

"Sure. But it can be booked up this time of year if you don't have a reservation."

"Oh, yeah, I forgot about the holidays."

"But I could teach you."

"You?" She wasn't too sure about this. "Don't you have your job here — I mean caretaking?"

He chuckled. "Not as much as you might think."

"But the homeowners, would they be bothered if you spent time with a guest? I wouldn't want you to jeopardize your job."

"I happen to be on great terms with the homeowner. He won't mind a bit."

"Seriously?" She studied him. Was he overstepping his bounds here? And yet something about him just made her want to trust him. He seemed like a regular good guy. "So you're a good skier?"

"Good enough to teach a beginner like you." He grinned.

"Well, that might solve the problem with Harris. I know Gillian will throw a serious fit if I spend too much time with him."

"And she won't mind if you spend time with the caretaker." He led her back into the mudroom.

Emma shrugged. "Oh, she'll probably mind. But not in the same sort of way. And anyway, it might be good for her."

"How's that?"

"I shouldn't say this, but Gillian can be . . . oh, you know, a little snooty. It's sort of how she was raised. Underneath all that, she's okay. But I'll warn you, she can come across as superficial and materialistic at times."

"And you're not?"

Emma laughed. "No way. I substitute teach for a living. You can't be materialistic on my meager salary." She wanted to add that it was probably about the same as his but didn't want to insult him.

"And yet you're friends with Gillian and her family?"

"It's a long story." She sighed. "And sometimes — not always — well, it kind of feels like they need me. I know that's weird, and it probably sounds egotistical, like I think I'm something special. But it's not like that. I just think I help bring them down to earth."

"Well, you probably need to get back to them. I have some, uh, caretaking things to take care of. But if you want your free skiing lesson, meet me down here at eight. The lift opens at nine, and we'll want to make fresh tracks."

"Fresh tracks?"

"You know, the first ones down the slope. Beat the rush."

"Oh . . . yeah. You're sure your boss won't mind?" she asked again.

"Positive. Part of being a good caretaker is taking good care of the guests." He grinned as he picked up a random ski pole and dropped it into a barrel. "Here at eight and don't be late."

"It's a date." She felt her cheeks warm. "Not really a date. I mean, I was just trying to rhyme with you."

He laughed. "I like that. A girl who can rhyme."

She promised to meet him here the next morning then, returning to the laundry room, Emma gathered up a few things she hoped would appease Mrs. Landers and took them into the now quiet house. She wasn't sure where the guys were, but she'd overheard Grant telling Harris that he wanted to visit a nearby brewery. So it seemed, for the moment, she had this marvelous house all to herself, and she intended to fully explore it. Whoever owned this place wasn't just wealthy, they seemed to have good taste too. Everything about this place felt so right. At least to her. She knew Gillian's mom had her own opinions. But to Emma, this house was perfection. And its caretaker wasn't bad either.

SEVEN

West didn't know what it was about that girl . . . but something about Emma had gotten under his skin. Sure, she was pretty. Almost exotic looking with that long, glossy black hair, espresso-colored eyes, and fine features. But it was more than just looks. She had a quiet gentleness about her. Sort of peaceful and calming. A quality he didn't often see in women. Especially in beautiful women. Especially in women who discovered his true identity. Once a girl found out he was TW Prescott, one of the "most successful songwriters of his generation," not to mention best buddies with Gunner Price, the games would begin. And they were games he wasn't good at playing. As a result, he tended to avoid dating in general.

So when he called his mom later that night, he wasn't quite sure what to tell her. "Something has come up here, Mom," he began. "I might not make it out tomorrow."

"The weather?"

"Well, the weather is one thing. But it's something more."

"Is it the house-swap guests?" she asked with concern. "I had a feeling this wasn't a good idea, but Drew was so certain. And I must admit this home is pretty gorgeous. The boys have sure enjoyed that pool. But if the Arizona guests are a problem, I'm so sorry."

"Not a problem exactly." He didn't want to say too much. "But I think I'll be waylaid at least one more day — maybe two."

"But you'll be here by Christmas Eve?"

"That's my goal. As long as I can get a flight."

"I sure hope this house swap hasn't ruined your Christmas, West. Where are you staying anyway?"

"In my studio."

"On that Murphy bed?"

"It's not bad."

"Well, hopefully you'll get it all taken care of quickly. Just keep me posted."

"I will, Mom." As he hung up, he felt a twinge of guilt. It wasn't that he'd lied to his mother, but he hadn't told her the whole truth. He was usually more honest with his mother than anyone, but he'd held back for a couple of good reasons. First of all, he didn't want to worry her about not making it to Arizona in time for Christmas. Even more than that, he didn't want her to get her hopes up. He knew how she wanted him to find just the right girl. She worried that he was becoming a hermit or a lonely "confirmed bachelor" who would never marry and give her more grandchildren.

If his mother realized he'd delayed his travel plans for Emma, she would jump to conclusions. But West's track record with women wasn't impressive. For some reason he usually attracted the wrong ones, "gold diggers" as McKenzie liked to call some of them. Unfortunately, West had fallen for a pretty face before . . . and the outcome had been disappointing. Not only to him but his whole family. It was possible that he was wrong again — and he didn't want to drag everyone down that path one more time.

"It's too early to go to bed," Gillian told Emma as they sat around the big rock fireplace where a large log was still burning. "It's barely ten. Didn't you get the memo? This is vacation. We stay up late and sleep in. Remember?"

"That's right," Harris agreed. "Don't bail on us, Emma."

"Yeah," Grant chimed in. "No party poopers allowed on this vacation."

Emma smiled patiently as she leaned against the tall log post. "But I heard Gil saying that being on vacation means you get to do whatever you want — isn't that what you said when your parents turned in?"

"That's because we *wanted* them to go to bed," Gillian told her.

"But you get to stay up late with the grownups." Grant grinned.

"I appreciate that, but I'm tired, and I have to get up early for a ski lesson in the morning."

"Seriously?" Gillian blinked. "You already booked a lesson? You work fast, girl."

Emma just nodded, not eager to confess she'd agreed to let the caretaker give her a lesson. She could just imagine Gillian's reaction. Especially since she'd already expressed her opinions on the guy.

"Is it a private lesson?" Grant asked with interest. "Or can I come along? I need to brush up on some skills."

"Oh, I thought Harris was going to help you," Emma said lightly. Hopefully, Harris would take the hint that she didn't want a lesson from him.

"Good point. I'm not sure I want anyone besides Harris to witness me flopping in the snow like a fish outta water." He turned to

Harris. "You okay with that?"

"Sure. But I'd like an early start. I want to hit that fresh powder before it's all torn up by other skiers and riders."

"What do you consider an *early start*?" Grant frowned.

"The lifts open at nine. So we should probably head out around eight or even earlier since we'll need to rent skis for the week. Might be good to beat the rush."

Grant let out a groan. "So much for sleeping in."

"Well, anyway, I'm calling it a night," Emma announced again. "See you all in the morning."

"You won't be seeing *me* in the morning," Gillian said. "I'm on vacation."

"Emma's got the right idea." Harris stood. "I'm hitting the hay too."

"Yeah, guess I'll call it a night." Grant conceded.

"Killjoys!" Gillian yelled out. "You guys are a bunch of party poopers!"

"Good night, Gillian dear," Emma called back sweetly. She knew it was pointless to engage with her right now. Hopefully she'd be in better spirits in the morning . . . or afternoon by the time she got up.

Emma hadn't said much about her sleeping quarters, but she still felt certain she'd scored the best room in the house. It wasn't fancy in the way that Gillian or her mom would appreciate, and Gil wouldn't like the lack of closet space. But to Emma, it was perfect. The fabulous view had only gotten better as the sky turned dusky earlier. While alone in the house, Emma had just stared in wonder as the sunset transformed the snowy slope into shades of indigo blue and purple. Meanwhile the lights from the nearby ski lodge had glowed like golden torches. It had been absolutely magical.

It was still magical. So magical that she didn't want to close the blinds. She got ready for bed in the bathroom then, snug in the big bed, she looked out the window, happily drifting to sleep with the gorgeous view still imprinted in her mind.

EIGHT

Emma woke early the next morning. Eager to put on the ski clothes she'd gotten last week in Phoenix, she just hoped she'd chosen correctly. According to the sales girl who'd helped her — and who'd vetoed some of Gillian's less practical suggestions — Emma should have exactly what she'd need for the slopes. Even though Emma had only chosen from the markdown rack, which Gillian had made fun of, it had stretched Emma's budget. She'd rationalized that a ski vacation in Colorado was worth it. Hopefully, she wasn't wrong.

"You're up early," Mr. Landers said when Emma went into the kitchen. "I just made coffee. Want some?"

"I'd love some." She ran her hand over the granite countertop.

"Looks like you're going to hit the slopes." He handed her a steaming mug, then frowned. "But the boys already took off.

Were they supposed to wait?"

"No. That's okay." She took a sip. "I'm having a private lesson this morning. I'm such a beginner — it seemed like a good idea."

"Well, I hope you have fun. And be safe. I want to get up there too, but maybe not today. I promised to stick around with Lisa." He filled another mug with coffee. "And I promised to bring her coffee in bed too."

"I hope she slept well."

"Well, she'll probably complain," he said. "But I heard her snoring. I think those pillows and things you found helped. Thanks, Emma." He grinned. "It's nice that you could come up here with us. Have a great day." He held up the two mugs. "I better get back to my lady."

Emma wasn't very hungry, but it wasn't eight yet, and she knew she'd probably need something to give her energy. She ate a yogurt and half a muffin then went out to the mudroom to discover West wasn't there yet. Hopefully he wasn't going to stand her up. Well, unless this was something he shouldn't be doing. She didn't know what the rules were for caretakers of beautiful homes like this, but he'd seemed pretty laidback. She waited a bit, then returned to the

76

kitchen for a second cup of coffee.

As she carried it back, she wondered if West might be one of those guys who worked as little as possible in order to ski as much as they could. Hopefully she hadn't been mistaken to trust him. He seemed nice enough, but who knew? Gillian certainly hadn't approved of him . . . but then Gillian didn't approve of a lot of things that Emma liked.

"Good morning." West popped into the room with a big smile, but he was still wearing jeans and the same flannel shirt from yesterday.

"Good morning." She stood. "Are we still on for today?"

"You bet." He looked at the coffee mug. "Any more of that?"

"Sure. Want me to get you some?"

"Yeah, thanks."

West followed her into the kitchen, and as she filled a mug, he helped himself to one of the muffins sitting on the counter. They'd been left by the homeowner, along with some fruit and a few other staples. Perhaps that was part of the caretaker's job.

"Where is everyone?" he asked, looking around.

She explained the others' whereabouts as he doctored his coffee with cream and sugar. He obviously felt comfortable in this house and seemed to know where everything was located. "Nice ski togs," he said with a crooked grin.

"Really? Or is something wrong?"

"No, I'm serious. They look like good choices. Especially for a beginner."

"Meaning?" Why did she feel he was teasing her?

"Meaning nothing, Emma." He smiled. "You look great. And if you'll excuse me for a minute, I need to check something in the laundry room."

Emma wasn't sure what to make of him, but it was comforting to see his familiarity with this house. She'd actually wondered if he could be an imposter. But he clearly seemed to be the caretaker.

When West came back into the kitchen, he had on a different plaid flannel shirt, but she decided not to mention it. "Ready to get going?" He set his mug in the sink.

"Whenever you are. I heard it's good to get there early to rent skis." She put the two mugs in the dishwasher.

"Oh, you're not renting skis. Come on, I think we can get you set up." He led her back to the mudroom. "As long as your feet aren't too big or too small. What size are you anyway?"

"Eight," she said hesitantly.

"Eight is great." He picked up a pair of boots from the ones lined up on a high shelf. "These should work just fine."

"But don't they belong to the home-owners? I don't think we should just —"

"It's okay." He handed them to her.

"But I don't want you to get into trouble, West. I don't mind renting something at the lodge and —"

"You won't find anything as good as these for rent."

"But the homeowners might not —"

"Don't worry, it's okay." He grabbed a good-looking pair of boots for himself, setting them by the door, and then selected skis and poles, as well as goggles and a few other items that he put into a small duffel bag. "You take this and your boots and we'll start loading up." After a couple of trips, the skis were snapped onto the roof rack on top of the Jeep and everything else was stowed in the back. "Let's go," he said.

Emma felt uneasy as she got into the Jeep. It seemed West was a little too comfortable in his employer's house. "Are you sure it's okay to use all this stuff?" she asked as he drove down the snowy street. "I don't want you to get into trouble or —"

"Trust me, it's fine. My boss and I are

like this." He crossed his fingers with a mischievous grin.

"Okay." She still wasn't convinced, but she decided to take in the scenery instead. "This place is so beautiful," she said as he drove through the quaint little town. "I can't imagine what it would be like to live here."

"It's pretty great."

"Was it the skiing that brought you here?"

"Pretty much. It's nice to drive just a few minutes then hit the slopes."

"Have you lived here for long?"

"Well, I've lived in Colorado for most of my life, except for a few years in Nashville, but I couldn't wait to get out of there and back here. It was my dream to live in Breckenridge."

"And to be a caretaker?" she asked.

He chuckled. "Now that's a funny dream."

"Well, if it allows you to ski as much as you like . . ."

"Good point. And I do get to ski almost as much as I like. But I have to work sometimes." He parked. "Here we are." He got out, and after helping Emma into her boots and borrowed goggles and gloves, he showed her how to carry her skis and poles. They walked toward the lodge. Rather, he walked, she sort of bumbled.

"Oh, wow." She paused to gape at the

80

slope. "That's so high, West. Are you sure I'll be able to do this?"

"Sure, this place has some of the best beginner slopes around. Lots of people come here to learn."

"Really?" She started to walk and then stumbled, dropping her skis. "I can barely walk."

"Don't worry, skiing is easier than walking with this stuff." He grinned. "Why don't you wait out here while I get your pass."

"I'll give you some money." She fumbled with a glove, ready to retrieve the cash she'd stashed in a pocket, but he stopped her.

"My, uh, boss, he has a special deal with the lodge. Your pass is free this week."

"Oh?" She blinked. "Okay, then great. Thanks." As she waited outside, she studied the slopes and wondered about West's generous boss. Was the pass actually free? Had Harris and Grant gotten free passes too? But then West came back, and after attaching the pass to her parka, he began to lead her out into a less busy area.

"We'll get you set up here and you can practice a little before we head for the beginner chair." He showed her how to hold her poles, then knelt down to help guide her boots into the skis. "My best advice to you right now is just relax."

"Okay." She squinted up at the gleaming slope. "It's bright."

"Let me help you with your goggles." He slipped them into place. "Now let's move a little. Try to feel how the skis move on the snow with just your body weight. Try to relax and just naturally follow the motion. Sort of go with the flow."

"Uh-huh." She tried to do what he said, but she barely moved. "Go with the flow."

"Yeah. That's it."

"This is fun," she said as she continued to slide through the snow, increasing speed with him right next to her. "But if I get going too fast, how do I slow down? Or stop?"

"You want the beginner's brakes?"

"Of course, I'm a beginner," she declared.

"Just remember to relax. If you get all tense, it will be harder."

"Okay. But tell me how to stop."

"Watch me." He moved ahead of her then pulled the tips of his skis together. "This is snowplowing and a beginner's easiest way to stop. You just dig in your heels and push outward. Not too much."

She did as he said, and to her amazement, she slowed down and eventually came to a complete stop. "Wow, that does work."

"You're a fast learner." He grinned.

"Or you're a good teacher." She smiled

back. "Thanks."

He helped her practice going and slowing and stopping then explained how to catch a chairlift. "Again, the important thing is to relax. But be ready." And just like that they were going up the hill.

"This is so great," she told him. "I think I'm going to love skiing."

"Well, it's a little early to say for sure, but I have a feeling you're going to be a natural. I can tell you're athletic."

"And I've always liked a challenge."

"Well, hopefully, you won't mind taking a tumble or two. That's just par for the course."

"I figured as much."

"But if you stay relaxed, falling's a lot less painful. Kind of like life."

"That makes sense." She looked up the mountain. "It's so beautiful here — I can hardly believe this place is for real. You're so fortunate to live here, West. I'd happily become a caretaker to live here."

He laughed. "Well, who knows, maybe we can find you a position. And speaking of position, let's get you ready to get off this thing." He told her to slide to the edge of the chair and how to hold her poles. "When your skis come in contact with the snow, you will stand up and let the chair gently push you. Then just keep going."

"Okay." She took in a deep breath then did as he said, and once again it worked. "This is easier than I expected."

He adjusted his goggles. "Well, it's about to get a little harder, but I have a feeling you'll manage just fine."

She looked down the hill and slowly nodded. "Okay. Remind me what to do next."

"Stay relaxed. Keep your skis parallel — until you need to slow down. Then just snowplow like we practiced. In fact, you should probably start out with a little snowplowing. Just to give you a feel for the slope. It's surprising how a slight incline can really get you going. You want to control it."

"Yes . . . control it." Like she hadn't been trying. "I think I'm ready."

"I'll just ski behind you. That way I won't distract you."

"Okay, if you think that's best."

"Yep. Take off when you're ready."

Following his instructions, Emma started out with the snowplow position and then slowly let herself go faster . . . and then faster. It was incredibly fun — and exciting. Until she saw a couple of kids straight ahead of her. "How do I turn?" she yelled as she tried to slow down by snowplowing. She heard him yell something, but it was too late — she splatted onto the snow with skis and poles all over the place.

"Are you okay?" He stopped fast right next to her, leaning down.

"Other than my hurt pride, I'm fine." She chuckled. "That was fun. Not the falling part. The skiing part."

He helped her up and back into her skis, then explained a bit about turning. "It's all about the weight of your body and your leg strength." Standing in place, he demonstrated how to lean right and left. "Follow me over to this gentle slope and we'll practice it together."

She followed him, and after a few runs and one small tumble, she thought she was getting the hang of it. By the time they got down the hill, she was ready to go up again. "Do you mind hanging with me on the beginner slope?" she asked as they rode the lift again.

"Not at all."

"But I know you must want to do some more challenging runs. I mean, that's why you're here, right?"

"Sure, but I can do that anytime. I promised you a lesson, and you're going to get it. You don't think you've graduated West's Beginner Ski School, do you?"

She laughed. "Not hardly."

For the next couple of hours they went down the beginners' slopes, and when West insisted it was lunchtime, Emma felt like she'd gotten the hang of it. "That is the coolest thing I've ever done," she said as they walked over to the lodge. "Seriously, I love skiing."

"I was right. You're a natural. I'm guessing before it's time to go home to Arizona, you'll be taking on some of the challenging runs."

"And then I won't want to go home."

"Aren't there ski areas there?"

"I guess so. I think Harris or Grant mentioned a ski area. I just never thought much about it before." She pointed ahead to an outdoor dining area. "Speaking of Grant and Harris, I think I see them over there."

"Did you want to join them?"

"Not particularly." She held her head down, hoping they wouldn't notice her, but it was too late. Grant was already standing and waving. She held up her hand in a lackluster wave.

"Come here," he called.

Emma braced herself as she introduced West to the guys, careful not to mention he was the caretaker. "West is the best ski instructor ever," she bragged as they sat down. "He had me skiing just like that. And

I've only fallen down a few times."

"And after lunch she'll graduate to an intermediate chair," West told them as he waved down a waiter.

"Sounds like you're doing better than I am," Grant said glumly. "At the rate I'm going, I'll probably be crippled by the end of the day. Maybe I should take lessons from West too."

"There's an idea," Harris said. "How about if we do a swap. West could take you on some beginner runs and I'll see how well Emma does on an intermediate run."

Before Emma could object, the guys seemed to have put together a plan. As she perused the lunch menu, she wondered what Grant would think when he discovered it was the caretaker giving him skiing lessons. Hopefully, West wouldn't mind. And who knew? Maybe it was just part of the caretaker's job to care for the guests on the ski slope too.

NINE

West wasn't too sure about this new skiing arrangement, but before they parted ways after lunch, he exchanged phone numbers with Emma. "In case you need me," he quietly told her. "Or if you want another lesson."

"Thanks." Her dark eyes twinkled as she punched his number into her phone. "It's nice of you to help Grant like this. I'm sure he'll appreciate it."

"Don't forget what I taught you," he said. "Staying relaxed helps. But don't lose control. The intermediate slopes are a lot steeper than what you've been on. You should probably traverse."

"What's that?"

"Cut swaths across the hill by going back and forth." He used his hand to demonstrate. "That helps you to go down more slowly, with more control."

She nodded with a look that said she was

taking his advice seriously. "Did you use to teach skiing or something?" She put her goggles on.

"Just to friends and family. And most of them weren't as easy to teach as you." He remembered the first time he'd tried to teach McKenzie to ski — it had been painful. His nephews caught on much faster.

"Come on, Emma," Harris called out. "Let's see what you got."

West watched as Emma went over to join him. Instead of waiting for her to catch up, Harris shot over to the chairlift, with Emma slowly trailing him. Hopefully, Harris didn't expect too much from her. The guy had seemed a little full of himself, almost as if he had something to prove. Or maybe he just wanted to show off for Emma.

"You worried about Emma?" Grant asked as he caught up with West.

"Maybe a little. She did surprisingly well this morning, but she's still a beginner. I hope Harris won't push her too hard."

"You mean like he pushed me — like he wanted me to go right over a cliff." Grant rubbed his elbow as they got in line for the beginner lift. "I'm going to need the hot tub tonight."

"Or ice packs." West studied him. "Is this your first time skiing?"

"No, but I've only been a few times before, and I never got the hang of it then. Maybe skiing isn't for me."

West shrugged. "Or maybe you just need a good teacher."

"Or a good physical therapist." Grant looked nervous as they moved up the lift line.

"My theory is that you need to relax to ski well. Have you heard that before?"

"Not really. Harris just shouts directions at me, so it's been hard to take it all in, let alone relax."

Once they reached the top of the slope, West began to give Grant the exact same instructions he'd given Emma. Okay, it wasn't nearly as much fun, but he actually felt a little sorry for this guy. Grant was obviously not as athletic as Emma, and Harris had probably made him feel even less so. But Grant was good-natured, and with each tumble, he'd crack a joke and crawl back to an upright position.

"That wasn't too painful." Grant brushed snow off his chin. "Maybe that whole relaxation bit helps."

Their second run was better, and Grant only fell once. By the third run, Grant was much improved but not nearly as good as Emma. As he finished the run, West wondered how she was doing. Was Harris being too hard on her? As he waited for Grant to make his way down, West checked his phone to see that Emma had texted him. She wanted to meet up.

"Emma wants to meet us for a break." West held up his phone. "In about fifteen minutes. But we probably have time for another quick run."

"Nah, I'm due for a break — before I break a bone." Grant turned to him with a smile then suddenly lost his balance and tumbled backward onto the hard-packed snow. "Guess I spoke too soon."

West chuckled as he held out a pole to help tug Grant to his feet. "You just lost your focus for a moment."

"Yeah, along with my self-respect." Grant nodded to where a cluster of teenage girls were laughing at him.

As they skied toward the lodge, Grant pointed out a blonde in a fur-trimmed blue parka. "Guess we should go say hey to my sister — the resident snow bunny."

West suddenly remembered his unpleasant encounter with the Ice Princess yesterday. He wanted to think of some excuse to avoid a confrontation now but knew it was too late. She was waving them over. They removed their skis then Grant politely introduced him to Gillian. She smiled prettily until he took off his goggles. Then she tipped up her sunglasses, and her pale blue eyes stared at him with a perplexed look. "Aren't you the caretaker?" she finally said.

"No, he's a ski instructor," Grant told her. "And he's good."

"I'm also, uh, the caretaker of the house you're staying in," West told Grant.

"No kidding?" Grant peered curiously at him as he peeled off his gloves.

"Yep. It's my job to keep that house running in tip-top condition." Really, wasn't that the truth? West worked to pay the bills and hire maintenance people. In a way, he was the actual caretaker. Just not in the way they were imagining.

"Well, you're still a good ski instructor." Grant sat down. "He could teach you a thing or two, Gillian."

"No, thank you." She dipped a finger into the whipped cream on top of her hot drink. "I am just here to enjoy the view. By the way, where's Emma?"

"Harris insisted on taking her on the intermediate slope," Grant explained. "Where he tried to kill me. Hopefully Emma will survive."

"But this is Emma's first day," Gillian said. "Is she ready for that?"

"Ask West. He was her instructor this morning." Grant picked up the drink menu.

Gillian turned to West. "Is she ready for that?"

"Why don't you ask her yourself?" He nodded to where Harris and Emma were quickly approaching. Harris did a fast stop, shooting snow up as he did. Emma slowed down by snowplowing. But as she got out of her skis and removed her goggles, West could tell she wasn't happy.

"How did it go?" He went over to help her park her skis and poles.

"Horribly," she said quietly. "I fell down about ten times on the first run."

"And after that?" They walked over to the table where Harris was already seated.

"A little better." She made a face at Harris. "I think you wanted to kill me up there."

Grant laughed. "Now you know how I felt, Emma."

"I never should've traded ski partners with you," Emma told him.

"I'm glad you did. West is a great teacher."

"And did you know he is the *caretaker* for the house we're staying in?" Gillian said in a tone that sounded a bit catty. "A man of many talents."

"No kidding? That's your real job — tak-

93

ing care of a house?" Harris looked unimpressed.

"Well, if West needed another job, he'd do well as a ski instructor." Emma sounded defensive, which West thought was sweet. "Unfortunately, I didn't have enough lessons to keep up with Mr. Hotdog Harris." She frowned at Harris. "And I've got the bumps and bruises to prove it."

"Sorry 'bout that." Harris held up his hands with a sheepish grin. "I guess I got carried away up there. But it's only because I wanted to do some *real* skiing today. The snow is awesome, and it's hard maintaining a slow pace all the time. I'm overdue for a real good run. But you beginners seem to need —"

"Hey, why not ski with me?" West suggested. "I'm ready to go after it."

"Sure about that? Can you handle a good tough run?"

West smiled. "No problem. But I'm not sure what you consider a good tough run. I mean, some consider Lulu a challenge, but I prefer Needle's Eye because you really have to work for it. But if you're super experienced and like to billy-goat down, we could take on Nine Lives. It just depends on how good *you* are. Totally your call. I wouldn't want to push you past your comfort zone."

Harris laughed as he stood. "Man, I wish someone *would* push me. You're on, Mr. Caretaker Dude. Let's go grab a drink then do this."

West slowly stood. "We'll probably be gone awhile. So I guess I'll see you guys later." He directed this mostly to Emma. That was his one regret, not getting to spend more time with her. But Harris needed a ski buddy — and he was about to get one!

West hoped Harris was as good as he claimed. Otherwise a tough run would be too much for him. In a way, West could relate to Harris's impatience. He was ready for a good hard run himself. He just wished he'd had a chance to see Harris's skiing skills first. He didn't like the idea of seeing anyone — not even someone as arrogant as Harris — coming down on a stretcher.

TEN

West and Harris had barely left before Gillian started in. "I cannot believe you guys have gotten all buddy-buddy with the hired help."

"Is that a problem?" Emma didn't want to hear Gillian rag on West. Especially since she was still disappointed that Harris had snatched him away.

"Seriously?" Gillian scowled. "Don't you think it's a little weird? After all, we're guests in the home he works for — I mean, he's like the yard boy. He is literally the janitor, Emma."

"And he's literally a nice guy." Emma had expected Gillian to react but wasn't prepared for so much animosity.

"He's the caretaker."

"You say that word like it's something terrible —"

"You know what I mean, Emma." Gillian gave her the look. "He shovels snow for a

96

living — anyway, he's supposed to. He's not even a good caretaker."

"The place seems pretty well cared for to me," Grant said lightly.

"Whatever." Gillian rolled her eyes. "My point is that you guys shouldn't befriend the hired help. He's a maintenance man."

"And a durned good ski instructor," Grant countered.

"But he's the caretaker." Gillian sipped her drink.

"He's both," Emma clarified. "And he's a good guy."

"I have to agree with Emma on that. He might be a caretaker, but he's cool. I like him, Gillian. So get off your high horse and cut the guy some slack." Grant excused himself to get a snack.

"Ditto to what Grant just said." Emma sipped her tea.

"But what kind of career is *that*?" Gillian demanded. "I mean, he's got to be our age, or older. And he's a caretaker? What's up with that?"

"Well, it's really none of our business, but I think he takes care of the house in order to ski."

"So he's a ski bum."

"What difference does it make to you what he is?" Emma said, irritated. "Why do you even care?" She knew she should be more gracious to Gillian. After all, she was Gillian's guest. But still . . . Gillian needed a crash course in good manners.

"Because you're my friend and Grant is my brother and I don't get it."

"Well, he helped me get the hang of skiing." Emma decided to change topics by telling Gillian about the fun she'd had skiing.

"But then you skied with Harris?" Gillian's brows arched. "How was that?"

"Like I already said, Harris pushed me too hard."

"Me too." Grant sat down with a bag of chips and a soda.

"It was more fun to ski with West," Emma admitted.

"That's for sure." Grant rubbed his shoulder.

"Well, it's probably because Harris is a better skier than the caretaker." Gillian's smile looked smug. "I hope he doesn't push our caretaker too hard. Who will shovel the snow?"

Grant opened a brochure, pointing to the map. "Here are the runs West mentioned. Needle's Eye and Nine Lives and whatever the other one was. According to the descriptions, those are considered the hardest slopes."

"Hopefully they'll make it down in one piece." Emma didn't want to think how Harris might goad and push West up there. And yet, West was sensible and easygoing, and probably more experienced than Harris. West would be just fine. She hoped.

Emma gently elbowed Grant. "Hey, you, feel like taking on the easy slope with me, or are you all worn out and ready to play snow bunny with your sister?"

"Do I look like a snow bunny?" He crumpled the empty chip bag. "It might help my confidence to do a few more easy runs." He frowned. "Well, as long as you don't show off by skiing circles around me — like Harris did."

"Ha — I barely know how to turn." Emma laughed.

"I'll get our skis ready," he said.

Emma forced a smile for Gillian. "In the meantime, I'm guessing you'll hang out here sipping cocoa and looking adorable."

"Thank you." She touched up her lip gloss and smoothed her hair.

"So you don't mind being abandoned?"

"Not at all," Gillian said pleasantly. "My chances of attracting some wealthy entrepreneur improve when I'm alone."

"Right." Emma put on her goggles. "So are you giving up on Harris then?"

"Not at all. And I'm relieved to find out you don't like skiing with him."

"That's for sure." Emma tugged on her gloves. "I hope I never ski with him again — I'll go out of my way to avoid it."

"I wish you'd avoid that caretaker too," Gillian said. "Besides the fact he's not in your league, it's not fair to Grant."

Emma wanted to straighten her out on both points but knew it was useless. "Don't worry yourself, Gil, I have no intention of getting involved with West. I just happen to appreciate the ski lessons." Hiding her irritation, Emma simply waved and went over to where Grant was struggling to get into his skis. Apparently, he hadn't gotten a lesson from West on how to do it gracefully. She explained, showing him how to align his skis and plant his poles then neatly step in. "See," she held out her arms. "Easy breezy."

He imitated her method, then smiled. "You're the perfect ski buddy, Emma. And I know you won't laugh if I fall on my face."

"Hopefully you won't do that." She took off, moving toward the chairlift with Grant trailing behind her. She hoped he hadn't misread her invitation to ski together as anything more than mere friendship. Sort of like West and Harris now skiing together — except those guys didn't seem to be on friendly terms. Hopefully, they'd have a good time anyway. Emma didn't like to imagine them in a skiing showdown. But if it did turn into competition, her money was on West.

West tried to talk Harris into an easier run, but Harris stubbornly insisted on Nine Lives. "You need to be aware this is one of the toughest runs on the mountain," West warned him. "It's wicked steep."

"Are you saying it's too much for you?" Harris asked. "Chickening out on me?"

"Not at all. I just want you to be aware of how steep it will be."

"I like steep runs," Harris said as they got in line for the lift.

"Then you're gonna love this." West chuckled.

"And it'll be worth bragging rights." Harris continued to chatter at West as they rode up, talking about other places he'd skied and his favorite runs. But the higher they went, the quieter Harris became. When they got off the lift and West informed him that they still had a fifteen-minute hike to the top, Harris looked uneasy.

"The hike helps to get you warmed up for the run." West put his skis and poles over his shoulder. "Let's get going."

By the time they reached the top, Harris was huffing and puffing. "How high are we?" he asked breathlessly.

"Close to thirteen thousand feet." West paused to catch his breath. "Even if you live up here, it can catch you by surprise at times."

"Yeah, this is pretty high. Oh, wow!" Harris stopped to stare down at the sheer drop-off, and unless West imagined it, his tanned face seemed to pale. "That's seriously steep, man."

"You okay?" West asked him.

"Yeah." He nodded with a somber expression. "But I gotta admit, that looks pretty challenging."

"I told you it was one of Breck's toughest runs. But you said that's what you wanted." West checked his bindings then put his boots into them.

"Uh-huh." Harris put on his skis too.

West removed his water flask from his pack, taking a long swig. "So you're good at billy-goating?"

"Guess I better be. Don't have much choice, do I?" He turned to West. "And you say you've done this run before?"

West nodded. "Yeah. And it doesn't pull any punches. Like I told you, Nine Lives will definitely put you to the test."

"Do I need nine lives to survive it?" Harris wasn't smiling.

West laughed. "Nah, you can do this, buddy. Don't let it psych you out."

"You wanna go first?" Harris adjusted his goggles. "Kinda lead the way since you know this run."

"Good idea." West patted Harris on the shoulder. "Just take it easy, man, stay focused — and it doesn't hurt to pray." He grinned. "That helped get me down the first time."

"And you wanted to do it again?"

"Sure. I mean, you have to be in the right frame of mind. But every once in a while, I like the challenge."

"Uh-huh." Harris pulled his stocking hat down over his ears and nodded.

"And if your legs get tired or shaky, just holler down at me and we'll take a break."

"Okay." Harris stared down the steep slope. "Oh, man, oh, man."

"Here goes nothing." West took off and, blocking out all else, focused on the run.

After a lot of breaks and pep talks, they finally made it down. Harris was so tired, he could hardly walk. "My legs feel like rubber," he admitted as they paused outside the lodge.

"Looks like Emma texted me — in fact, a few times." West read her first message. "Uh-oh."

"What happened?"

"Grant broke his arm."

"You're kidding."

"Nope. Emma says he had a bad fall." He read the next text. "He was taken by ambulance to the hospital, and she and Gillian followed."

"That must've been fun." Harris pulled off his stocking hat, running his hand through his damp, messy hair.

"This last text says they just left the emergency room." He checked the time. "They're probably home by now. So I guess you'll have to ride back with me."

"As long as I don't have to walk." Harris shook his head. "How far away are you parked anyway?"

West laughed. "You can do it, buddy. Just think, you just made one of the steepest runs in Colorado — and you didn't break anything but a good sweat."

"And then Grant goes and breaks his arm on the bunny slope. Figures."

As West drove them home, he felt sorry for Grant and slightly amazed that it hadn't been Harris to suffer an injury. It had been obvious early on that Nine Lives was too much for him, but West had to give him credit for not giving up. Oh, he'd wanted to and had even asked about being rescued. But eventually they made it down, taking much longer than West would've on his own. At least they made it down before the sun set. That could've presented a serious problem.

But now West had a different problem. He needed to think of a way to tell his mother he wasn't leaving for Arizona until tomorrow. And he wasn't even sure about that. He still hadn't gotten enough time with Emma.

ELEVEN

Emma got a blanket from the linen closet and laid it over Grant. He was comfortably resting on the big leather sectional in the main living room with his arm propped up and a football game playing on TV. Meanwhile, Mr. Landers, in an effort to appease his wife, who was still in a foul mood, was fixing dinner. Gillian was unwinding in the hot tub. What she needed to unwind from was a mystery to Emma.

"I just can't believe it." Mrs. Landers was pacing again. "I knew it was a mistake to come to snow country. And on the very first day Grant nearly kills himself skiing."

"A broken arm is not life-threatening," Mr. Landers yelled from the kitchen.

"Yeah, Mom, don't worry so much," Grant said. "I'm not in any real pain. It's no big deal. Besides, Emma has been taking good care of me."

"But if we'd spent Christmas at home, this

never would've happened." Mrs. Landers was literally wringing her hands — making Emma feel even more guilty.

"I'm so sorry this happened," she told Mrs. Landers. "If Grant hadn't been —"

"It's not your fault, Emma," Grant interrupted. "I made a stupid mistake."

"Yes, but you were trying to help me."

"Which was ridiculous. You didn't need any help." He chuckled as he muted a commercial. "I did."

"That's just my point," his mother declared. "We are not a skiing family. Your father had no business doing this home exchange."

"Hey, I was having a good time skiing. And I think when my arm heals up and I get a bit more practice, I will become a fairly decent skier. So, Mom, if I'm not complaining, why are you?"

"Why am I?" Mrs. Landers blew out a frustrated sigh, then marched off toward her bedroom, muttering to herself about what a waste this trip had been.

"How about a fire?" Emma asked Grant, hoping to distract him from his mom's negativity. "That one last night was so cozy and warm."

He grinned. "Do you actually know how to make a fire in an old-fashioned fireplace?

I mean, I'm used to gas fireplaces where you push a button, and presto — flames."

"Who made the fire yesterday?"

"I don't know. It was going when we got here. Probably our caretaker."

She nodded. "Well, my parents' house happens to have an old-fashioned fireplace. It looks like there's enough wood right here to get one going. And I saw more firewood out by the garage."

"Great. I'd like to see a real Girl Scout in action."

Emma quickly got a fire started, then went outside to fetch more wood. She'd fully loaded the wood carrier when the Jeep pulled up. She waited as West and Harris got out, noticing that Harris seemed to be moving slowly.

"Are you okay?" she asked him. "Break any bones?"

"Just sore," he muttered. "Need hot tub."

She laughed. "Well, Gillian will be happy for some company. And afterward, you and Grant can commiserate over your battle wounds."

"Let me get that for you." West took the log carrier from her.

"Thanks." She noticed he still had some spring in his step as they all went into the house. Meanwhile Harris barely spoke to anyone and headed straight for the hot tub. West paused to stoke the fire, then loaded the rest of the wood into the heavy metal holder before going back for a second load and stacking it neatly as well. "This should keep you going for a while." He turned to Grant. "I hear you bailed."

"Huh?"

"Your wipeout. You know, when you fell and broke your arm."

"Oh, yeah." Grant nodded.

"So how you feeling?"

"Not too bad considering. But I'm bummed that I won't get to ski anymore this week. I was just getting the hang of it too."

"Yeah, you'd improved so much after our last lesson. I'm surprised you had such a bad fall."

"It was my fault," Emma confessed. "I was about to take a tumble when Grant tried to help me."

"Pretty dumb considering she remained upright and I totally ate it."

"It wasn't pretty." Emma cringed, remembering the awkward angle of his broken arm. "And I know it was painful."

"Tell me about it." He shook his head.

Emma frowned. "Yeah, but you held it together, Grant."

"You didn't hear me crying like a little girl when the paramedics loaded me into the ambulance." Grant slapped his forehead. "Crud! That reminds me."

"What's that?" she asked.

"I totally forgot about the car — the Prius that belongs to the house." He fished in his pocket and pulled out keys. "I used it to drive Harris and me to the lodge this morning. It's still parked over there."

West frowned. "Well, I guess I can take someone over there to get it."

Grant pointed to his cast. "Not me with this thing. And Gillian and Harris are in the hot tub. Dad's in the middle of —"

"I'll help you get it," Emma offered. She was eager to get out of the house. "Wait while I get my coat and boots."

"Right . . . and if no one minds, I need to get something from the master suite — for my boss. He, uh, forgot something up there."

"Oh?" Emma studied him, noticing he seemed uneasy. "But aren't the homeowners in Arizona? How will you get it there?"

"Next day air. No big deal."

"Oh, yeah. Well, I'm the one using that bedroom, but come on up." As she led the way upstairs, she warned him the room might be messy.

"That's okay. The homeowner isn't real tidy either." He entered the room with an amused expression. "The place looks pretty neat to me. Better than usual in fact." He pulled out a key ring and unlocked what appeared to be a walk-in closet. "My boss locked this up since it's got his personal stuff inside. I'll just be a minute or two." He went in and closed the door behind him.

As Emma pulled on her jacket, she wondered what his boss had forgotten that was important enough to go to this much trouble. Obviously, the homeowners trusted West since they'd given him a key to that closet.

West emerged with a large Nike duffel bag, then relocked the door. "All set."

"Your boss must've forgotten a lot," she said as they went downstairs.

"He's never been a very efficient packer." West chuckled as they went outside. "One summer he went to London and realized he'd forgotten to pack any shoes and all he had was the flip-flops he'd worn on the flight."

"So did you send him shoes?"

"Nah. He just asked the hotel concierge to shop for some for him."

"Well, he's obviously rich enough to do that."

She watched him toss the duffel into the back of the Jeep, and before long, they were driving through the charming downtown area. The quaint buildings were now glowing with strings of Christmas lights, and the old-fashioned golden streetlights reflected on the twilight-tinged snow. "It's so incredibly pretty here." She sighed as he stopped for a red light. "It's like driving through a beautiful Christmas card. Or a Hallmark Christmas movie."

He laughed. "Never heard that before."

"You're lucky to live here, West."

"I feel pretty blessed."

"Yes, *blessed* is a much better word for it. Seeing those mountains today . . . it made me think about God's creativity — to make such a beautiful world. And with so much diversity. I'll admit I haven't seen much of it — not in person — but I love watching travel shows . . . and imagining going someday."

"If you could travel anywhere, where would you go?"

"Anywhere?" She considered this. "Money's no object?"

"Sure. You just won the lottery. Where would you go?"

"I'd love to go to Switzerland . . . to see the Swiss Alps."

112

"Ah, good choice. The Matterhorn is magnificent."

"You've seen it?"

"Well, uh, obviously I've seen it in photos. Who hasn't?"

"But being here in Colorado — it must be nearly as good as the Swiss Alps, don't you think? So I'm not complaining."

"Do you think you'll still be into skiing? Even though Grant got hurt?"

"Of course. In fact, I didn't tell Grant, but I was sort of frustrated at him for getting hurt because I wanted to keep skiing. Pretty selfish, since it was sort of my fault."

"That's silly to blame yourself, Emma. Grant already admitted he'd blown it by trying to help you."

"Yeah, and then I had to lose the last couple hours of skiing."

West laughed. "You sound like a true-blue skier."

"I wish." She wondered how many Arizonans were serious skiers. Well, besides Harris. "So how did it go on Nine Lives?" she asked. "Harris looked pretty worn out."

He laughed even louder now. "I think old Harris bit off more than he could chew. I felt a little guilty for allowing him to take on the backcountry."

"Well, he asked for it."

113

West described some of their run. "Besides being worried that he could get injured, I actually felt sorry for him."

"Well, I'm glad he didn't get hurt, but I think it serves him right for being so hard on Grant and me. Now he knows how we felt."

West pointed to a brightly lit restaurant. "Hey, if you guys ever need a great place to eat — that's the spot."

"Bullwinkle's Dinner Club. Looks like fun."

"Want to go grab a bite?"

"Seriously? *Now?*"

"Why not? I know I'm starving after my last run."

"I'm pretty hungry too." She considered Mr. Landers making their dinner. He wasn't the greatest cook . . . but still. "I don't know."

"Bullwinkle's usually has some decent music going on. Especially during holidays."

"What kind of music?"

"Oh, something along the lines of folksy-country-bluesy." He chuckled. "That's probably not very descriptive."

"I actually get it. In fact, you're speaking my language. I like folksy-country-bluesy music myself."

"So how about it? Hey, there's a parking

spot right in front. It's calling to us."

"Okay! I'll text Gillian that I won't be home for dinner. I doubt they'll miss me anyway."

"Well, you're probably wrong about that. But I won't let you back out now."

Just like that they were going into a rustically charming restaurant that instantly felt familiar to Emma. Maybe it was the music. West hadn't exaggerated — it was very good. The food was even better. But West's company was the best. He was interesting and well versed on music — and just plain fun.

It would've been nice to linger longer, but Emma remembered the abandoned car at the lodge. "Shouldn't we go get it?" she asked West.

"I guess so." He sounded reluctant but motioned to the waiter to bring their bill.

"Dutch treat." Emma reached for her purse.

"No way." He waved his hand. "This one's on me." Before she could stop him, he handed the waiter his card — without even looking at the bill. She was tempted to point out that wasn't too smart but didn't want to be bossy. Instead, she thanked him and hoped he hadn't been overcharged.

"This place is great, and I totally loved

the music," she said as they left. Although she hadn't meant to, she started telling him about her own pursuit of music. "I actually gave up a couple of paying gigs to come to Colorado," she said as they got in the Jeep. "But I don't regret it."

"Seriously? You're a professional musician?"

She grinned. "Well, that would be stretching the truth. I'm a substitute teacher who aspires to be a musician, and once in a while I get paid to perform."

"So do you sing? Play an instrument? What?"

"I sing and accompany myself, primarily on guitar. Although I've been learning ukulele."

"Are you any good?"

She laughed. "My mommy and daddy think I'm very talented."

"Well, they're probably right. As soon as I met you, I could hear a melodic quality to your voice."

She laughed again. "Well, thank you . . . I guess." For a while they talked about music, realizing that they had similar tastes.

"So who are your favorite female performers?" he asked.

"Well, for old school, I like Emmy Lou Harris."

"Good choice."

"And Lucinda Williams. And I recently discovered Amanda Shires. Somebody told me I sound like her."

"Very cool. And how about your favorite male performers?"

"Hmm . . . well, I like Ed Sheeran. And Robert Ellis is good. And, of course, I love Gunner Price."

"Interesting." He turned into the mostly vacant ski lodge parking lot.

She heard her phone signaling a text. It was Gillian — demanding to know why Emma wasn't home yet.

"Everything okay?" he asked as he parked by the lonely blue Prius now dusted with snow.

"Gillian's irritated that I'm not back by now. Sounds like she and Harris want to use the Prius tonight." They both got out of the Jeep.

West dug a snow scraper from the trunk and began clearing the windows. "Why don't they use the SUV?" he asked her.

"I guess her dad said no. Gillian's not the best driver. Especially after dark."

"Great." West put the scraper in the back, then handed her the keys. "So Gil gets to drive the, uh, the homeowner's car?"

"I guess." Emma got into the driver's side.

"Thanks so much for dinner, West. I had a super evening." Even as she smiled, she felt sad underneath. She hadn't wanted it to end so abruptly. Especially since people had just started hitting the dance floor at Bullwinkle's. She would've liked a chance to dance with West.

TWELVE

West wasn't thrilled to hear that the Ice Princess — a bad driver — would be driving his Prius tonight. But what could he say? If she totaled it, at least it was covered. And the car was six years old anyway. Still, it was aggravating. Instead of going straight home, he decided to stop by the grocery store to replenish the basic necessities he kept in the studio's kitchenette. Unless his mother really insisted, West was determined to stick around throughout Christmas. He had to get better acquainted with Emma.

After putting the bags in the Jeep, he called his mother. He knew she'd be fretting over his absence and wasn't even sure what to tell her. Relieved that it went straight to voice mail, he left an apologetic message, insinuating that something regarding his house made it mandatory for him to remain there longer — which was true. Then he promised to get back to her by midday tomorrow. He knew she'd be disappointed. But if she understood the real reason for this delay, she would probably encourage him to stick around. Mom was always nagging him to find the right girl. From what he'd seen so far, Emma had all the right ingredients. Besides being beautiful, she was kind and gentle and sincere . . . and they shared many of the same interests. He felt certain his mom would approve.

When West got home, Gillian, Harris, and Emma were standing outside in front of the Prius. He parked his Jeep off to one side, leaving plenty of room for everyone to come and go then got out.

"Evening, folks," he called as he retrieved his grocery bags.

"Hey, West," Emma called back. "I was just telling these guys about Bullwinkle's Dinner Club — and the good food and music and dancing."

"And I was telling Emma she needs to go back there with us," Harris said. "But she's being very stubborn and refusing."

"Because I'm tired," Emma said.

"I'm not only tired, I'm achy and sore," Harris confessed. "But Gillian's making me go."

"Yeah, well, I feel sorry for leaving Grant here alone," Emma protested.

"He's not alone," Harris declared. "His parents are in there watching an old movie."

"I think it's very thoughtful that Emma wants to keep my poor brother company." Gillian used a sweet tone. "I'm sure he'll appreciate it. Especially since he got hurt trying to help her."

"I bet he's asleep by now. He just took a pain pill." Harris grabbed Emma's hand. "Come on, Em, we won't stay late. Just come and show us where this hot spot is located."

"She already told us." Gillian's tone turned impatient. "Let's just go, Harris. Time's a-wasting."

"Not without Emma." Harris opened the car door. "Come on, Emma, get in. No excuses. This is your vacation too."

"Well, if Emma comes, maybe we should make West join us too," Gillian said with arched brows. "That way she'll have someone to dance with."

"But West is probably tired too," Emma protested. "Why don't we just —"

"I'm not tired," he said quickly. "Just let me put this away and I'll be right back." Before anyone could protest, West stashed his provisions, then returned. "How about if I drive?" he offered.

"No," Gillian said sharply. "I'm driving

121

the Prius. You and Emma ride in back."

"My legs are too long for the back seat," West told her. "How about Emma and I take the Jeep and just meet you there?"

"Great plan!" Gillian gladly agreed.

As West drove back to the club, he asked Emma more about her music. "I've been wishing I could hear you do some music. Have you recorded anything?"

"No. I have a friend with a small studio. He keeps encouraging me to do an indie album — you know, to have something to sell at gigs — but I just can't afford it. Not yet."

"Yeah, it's not cheap to produce a decent indie. But I wish you had one, Emma. I'd love to hear you."

"I was tempted to bring my guitar up here, but Mr. Landers said to travel light."

"I can loan you a guitar."

"Really? You play guitar?"

He admitted that he played not only the guitar but a few other instruments as well. Still, he didn't say anything about songwriting. He liked that she still believed he was an impoverished caretaker. Going incognito allowed him to get acquainted with Emma on a level playing field. He didn't want her to be so impressed by his music career that she no longer wanted to tell him about her own. Or worse yet — although he couldn't imagine Emma acting this way — what if she tried to use him to launch her career? It wouldn't be the first time something like that had happened.

When they went into Bullwinkle's, Gillian was dragging Harris out to the dance floor. It wasn't long before West and Emma went out there too. Then after just one dance, Harris insisted they switch partners. Gillian looked irritated, but at least she didn't throw a full-blown fit over her new partner. West tried to treat her politely and couldn't deny she was a decent dancer, but when the song ended, he left her on the floor, heading straight for Emma. And so it went. He'd barely finish a dance with Emma before Harris would jump in and whisk her away — and West would get stuck with the Ice Princess again.

Finally, the band took a break, and while Emma visited the ladies' room and Harris went to refresh their drinks, West was seated at a table with Gillian, trying to think of a way to excuse himself. At least she was more interested in her phone than him. When the band's lead guitarist came over to introduce himself, shaking hands like they were old friends, West welcomed the distraction. "You guys are putting out some good music," he told the musician.

"Thanks, man, that means a lot coming from you."

"Oh, yeah." West instantly realized his mistake. This guy knew who he was. "Well, thanks for providing us with some extra good dance tunes tonight. Looking forward to some more. Your band's got a great beat." He spoke quickly as he stood, thinking he'd make a getaway before his cover was completely blown. Fortunately, Gillian was still glued to her phone.

"You still work with Gunner Price?" the guy asked with too much interest.

West mumbled an affirmative, hoping Gillian was still oblivious.

"Your songs are the best, TW. I write a little too, but nothing like your stuff. It's an honor to meet you. I heard you lived in Breckenridge, but I never dreamed I'd actually meet you in person."

"Yeah, well, I sort of need to go, uh, to check on something." West patted the guy on the back, then hurried away. Hopefully Gillian, distracted by her phone, had missed all that. But when the music started up again, and Harris and Emma weren't back, Gillian found West. Grabbing him by the hand, she grinned as she tugged him out to the dance floor with her. The Ice Princess had figured him out — he knew it.

Naturally, Harris used this opportunity to snag another dance with Emma. When Gillian refused to let West go for the next number, Harris got another dance with Emma. And another. Finally, West was fed up. The Ice Princess was a good dancer — and much friendlier than before — but he wanted to be with Emma.

"I need a break," he told Gillian. As they returned to their table, he didn't see Emma or Harris, not on the dance floor . . . or anywhere.

"Where'd they go — have you seen them?" he asked Gillian.

"Oh, Emma texted me a while ago. She's driving Harris home."

"What?"

"Yeah, I told her to just get the keys from my bag and use the Prius."

"But why?" he demanded. "Why did Emma need to drive him home?"

"Because Harris got a bad charley horse in his leg and could barely walk, let alone dance. It was probably from that treacherous slope you took him down today." She shook a finger at him with a sly smile. "Harris claims you tried to kill him."

"That's not exactly what happened." West was trying to wrap his head around this.

Emma took Harris home and now he was stuck here with the Ice Princess?

"I'm sorry, West, I should've mentioned it to you earlier. But we were having such a good time dancing." Her expression held a saccharine sweetness. "Who would guess that a caretaker has so many hidden talents?"

"Hidden talents?" He was trying to think of a way to put this evening to an end.

Her blue eyes twinkled. "Expert skier, expert dancer . . . makes me wonder what else you do expertly . . ."

"I'm a pretty good driver," he said wryly. "I can drive us home."

She stuck out her lower lip. "So you don't want to dance with me anymore? Just because Emma and Harris are gone?"

"It's late, Gillian. And I know you weren't too eager to dance with me —"

"Oh, that's just my little act. You should ask Emma about it. I always play hard to get around guys who interest me."

"Really?" He narrowed his eyes. "Why would I interest you?"

"Because you're so interesting." She laughed. "And after hearing everyone bragging about what a great ski instructor you are, I'm wondering if you'd have the patience to teach someone as uncoordinated

126

as me. I'm afraid I have two left feet."

"For two left feet, you're pretty good out there on the dance floor."

"Well, thank you." She beamed at him. "So there might be hope for me to learn to ski?"

"I'm sure there's hope. There's always hope. I've seen guys without legs ripping down a run."

She giggled. "So that's a yes — you *will* teach me to ski?"

"I, uh, I didn't say that." He glumly shook his head. "I know what you're doing, Gillian. And it's not working."

"What in the world do you mean?" She looked at him with wide, innocent eyes. He almost expected her to flutter her eyelashes but was glad she didn't.

"You know who I am." He stared intently at her.

"Sure. You're West, the multitalented caretaker of the house we're staying in."

"Right." He knew she was playing him. She had to be. "Well, just so you know it, Gillian, I don't like to play games."

"I totally understand. And I apologize for treating you so badly before. The truth is you hurt my feelings the first time we met. You have to admit you were a bit rude. For that reason, I wanted to punish you. But I am sorry about that. The more I've gotten to know you, the more I realize that there's a lot more to you than I thought. The others were right." She sighed. "I hope you can find it in your heart to forgive me."

He shrugged. "Sure, I forgive you. But like I said, I'm not into games. Besides that, I'm tired. So if you don't mind, I'd like to go home."

"I don't mind at all. Especially if we need to get up early tomorrow. You know, for my first ski lesson."

He didn't respond to this because he didn't want to hear her pleading or coaxing, but he had no intention of playing ski instructor to the Ice Princess tomorrow — or ever. Despite her innocent claims, he felt fairly certain she'd figured out his true identity. That had to be the only reason she was no longer treating him like something slimy stuck to the bottom of her fur-lined boots.

THIRTEEN

Emma couldn't understand the change that had come over her normally snooty friend, but it seemed that Gillian had suddenly decided West was just great. "He's even going to teach me to ski tomorrow," she proclaimed from the foot of Emma's bed.

"That's nice," Emma said groggily. "But if you don't mind, it's pretty late, and I'm sleepy."

"Well, we just got home. And I was so excited I had to talk to someone. I wanted you to know that I was totally wrong about West. *West . . .* isn't that a cool name?"

"Uh-huh." Emma yawned, leaning back into the pillows and wishing Gil would take the hint and go to bed.

"And we had so much fun dancing tonight. He's a good dancer. I get the feeling he's really into me, Emma. I just wanted to make sure you understood about that. You know, in case it was a problem for you. But you did assure me — just this afternoon — that your only interest in him was as a ski instructor, right?"

"Uh, yeah, right." Emma wanted to take her words back but knew it was pointless to dissuade Gillian from whatever it was she was trying to do. If Gil was determined to win West's attentions, let her. Emma felt pretty sure that a grounded guy like West would have little interest.

"Okay then." Gillian stood. "Good night, sweetie pie. Sorry to keep you up so late." She turned off the light and slipped out the door. But now Emma was wide awake — wondering if that conversation had been real or just a weird dream. Was Gillian seriously interested in pursuing a relationship with West — the caretaker? It made absolutely no sense.

Emma got out of bed and went over to look out at the snow-covered mountains, where a three-quarter moon illuminated them in an incredibly beautiful way. How would she feel if Gillian had fallen for West? And why wouldn't she? Emma certainly had fallen for him.

But had she really? Emma felt so confused. What was going on here? She ran this strange scenario round and round in her head, but she could not figure it out. Maybe

Gillian was playing some sort of game with Emma, trying to get her to confess to having feelings for the caretaker so that Gillian could set her straight. It wasn't out of the realm of possibilities when it came to Gillian. Still, it made no sense.

After a restless night, Emma eventually fell asleep — and didn't wake up until nine-thirty. She hurried to dress then went downstairs to talk to Gillian. Somehow she had to get to the bottom of last night's very strange conversation, which she felt sure must've just been a bizarre dream. But Gillian wasn't in her room. So Emma went down to the main floor where Grant was having coffee in the kitchen.

"Where's Gil?" Emma asked him.

"Brace yourself. My ski bunny sister got up early to go skiing." Grant shook his head in disbelief. "At least that's what Mom said. I still can't quite believe it."

"Seriously — skiing?" Emma blinked.

"Yeah, and listen to this if you really want to blow your mind. She went skiing with West — aka *the caretaker.*"

"Wow, that's definitely weird." Emma slowly filled a coffee cup. So it wasn't a dream. Gillian had flip-flopped on the social status of their caretaker.

"You're telling me. Remember the lecture

131

Gil gave us yesterday. What do you think happened to her? A head injury? Alien abduction and brainwashing?"

"Well, if Gil wants to learn to ski, she couldn't ask for a better teacher." Emma tried to sound nonchalant.

"Maybe so, but it's still bizarre."

"What's bizarre?" Harris came into the kitchen, reaching for a coffee mug.

"Well, it's bizarre that it looks like you're barely able to walk, old man." Grant laughed. "West sure took it out of you yesterday."

"I'll be okay." Harris stood straighter. "Just need to do some stretching and a little more time in the hot tub."

"But you're not skiing today?" Emma asked.

"I don't know. Maybe I am." He filled his coffee cup.

"How about you?" Emma pointed to Grant. "I know you're not skiing, but what are you up to?" She still felt a bit guilty for his broken arm.

"I'd kinda like to spook around town." He lowered his voice. "Mom and Dad are heading out to do some Christmas shopping, which reminded me I don't have anything for —"

"Hey, Gillian explicitly said no gifts since

we were supposed to pack light for this trip." Emma felt worried now — what if Christmas turned into a great big gift exchange? Mrs. Landers could be pretty extravagant sometimes.

"Yeah, that's what Dad told us, but you know how Mom always changes the rules. Anyway, I want to get a few things." He held up his cast-enclosed arm. "But I can't drive with this stupid thing."

"Want me to take you to town?" she asked halfheartedly.

His eyes lit up. "Would you mind?"

"Nah. Might be fun." She finished her coffee, setting the mug in the sink.

"Mind if I come too?" Harris asked hopefully.

"I thought you were going skiing." Grant frowned at him.

"Well, I still might go . . . later." Harris glanced at Emma. "Maybe you and I could ski this afternoon after we take our disabled buddy Christmas shopping."

Grant growled, holding up his cast like he planned to bean Harris, but Emma stepped between them. "Now, if you boys can't get along, no one will go shopping today," she teased in a maternal tone. "If I'm driving you, let's get going. I'd like to get in at least a couple hours of skiing this afternoon."

"Me too," Harris agreed. "How about if we finish up shopping in time to grab some lunch at the lodge? Then we'll be set to ski."

"What about me — what am I supposed to do then?" Grant asked.

"Maybe it's your turn to be the snow bunny today," Emma teased. "You can sit in the lodge looking all sweet and cute with your broken arm, sipping hot cocoa."

His eyes lit up. "Hey, I like that."

"So let's get this show on the road." Emma set her coffee mug in the sink. "Because I really *do* want to get in some skiing." Even more than she wanted to ski, she wanted to see Gillian and West with her own eyes. Then maybe she'd be able to make sense of this crazy new development.

West still didn't know how it had happened, how the Ice Princess had maneuvered to get him to give her ski lessons first thing this morning, but here they were on the bunny slope. "I thought you said Emma was going to join us," he told her after several runs, where she'd proved herself to be more coordinated than her brother.

"Well, I thought that was the plan." Gillian beamed at him as they boarded the chairlift again. "I'm sure that she and Harris were coming, but I haven't seen them anywhere. Have you?"

"No, but I know Emma was determined to get up here today. I can't understand why she's not —"

"Maybe she changed her mind. You know, it's a woman's prerogative." She laughed. "I do it all the time."

"But Emma said how much she loves skiing, and I was going to give her more lessons."

"Well, you are definitely a good ski instructor." She patted his shoulder.

"Maybe we should text them." West pulled out his phone.

"Let's do this run first." She pointed ahead. "It's almost time to get off."

"No problem." To prove this, he tucked his poles under his arm, texting Emma as he skied off.

"Oh, West." Gillian giggled. "You're such a show-off. If I tried that, I'd land on my face."

"Yeah, I don't recommend texting and skiing for anyone, particularly beginners." He continued to ski into position without the use of his poles. "But I'm being careful. My biggest concern here is having a novice skier plow into me."

"You mean like me?" She jutted out her lower lip.

"You're actually catching on pretty well. Let's see how you do on this run and then try to catch up with Emma and Harris." He tipped his head to her. "Okay, you go first."

"I'll try to remember everything you told me." She fluttered her eyelashes. "You really are a great ski instructor, West."

"You mean for a caretaker?" he taunted. "Or a ski bum?"

"Oh, West, I thought you'd forgiven me for my pettiness."

"Yeah, yeah. Okay, Gillian." He pointed to an open spot on the slope. "Your turn. Do your stuff and remember what I told you." He watched as she started down then checked his phone to discover Emma had already texted him back. Her response was a curt *shopping in town.* Nothing more. Almost as if she were giving him some sort of hint. But why? She'd seemed so friendly last night. He pocketed his phone and, keeping a safe distance from the beginners, zipped straight down the gentle slope, spraying snow as he reached Gillian at the bottom.

"You look like you know what you're doing," she teased. "What are you doing on the bunny hill?"

"Yeah, I'm wondering that myself." He scowled.

"What's up with you?" She blinked her big blue eyes like she thought he'd be impressed. "You look like you just lost your best friend."

"It's nothing." He held up his phone. "Except that I promised to call my family today."

Her brow creased. "Oh, are you planning to spend Christmas with them?"

"I'm not sure. But I promised to call them before noon. And you're right, I'm getting a little tired of the bunny slope. I need to hit a more difficult run — clear my head and stretch my legs." He forced a smile. "In the meantime, you go ahead and take a couple more runs here. You're doing well, but it'll be good practice for you to do it alone. We can meet up at the lodge later." And before she could protest, he skied off.

As he rode the lift up, he called his mom, and this time she answered. "What is going on?" she demanded. "I thought you'd be here by now, West."

"I'm sorry, Mom. Something came up."

"I know. That's what you keep telling me, but I'd like to know what it is that came up. Why aren't you here? Are you upset about the house switch?"

"No . . . not exactly." He gazed up at the mountain.

137

"What then?"

"Well, there's this girl."

"*Oh*? A girl?" Her voice suddenly softened. "Well, why didn't you say so sooner?"

"Because I wasn't sure about it. Everything happened pretty fast. And to tell you the truth, I'm starting to question it. I think she's giving me the cold shoulder."

"Well, then she's a very stupid girl."

"Oh, Mom." As he rode the lift, he told her about his scheme of playing caretaker and how Emma seemed so sweet.

"She sounds lovely. I wish I could meet her."

"She's a musician too." He shook his head. How'd he get in so deep — so soon? This wasn't a bit like him.

"And you're absolutely sure she doesn't know who you are, West?"

"I don't think so. But I'm not so sure about her friend." He told her about Gillian.

She laughed. "Sounds like you've got your hands full. Well, just do what you think is best. If you want to stay there, everyone here will understand. I just want you to be happy, West, and to have a good Christmas."

He wasn't sure that was even possible, but instead of admitting that, he thanked her and promised to keep her updated. As they said goodbyes, he got off the chairlift. Standing at the top of the slope, he said a silent prayer. If this thing with Emma was the real deal — and meant to be — he prayed that it would work out.

Flummoxed wasn't a word she normally used in everyday conversation, but that's how Emma felt as she explored the charming Breckenridge shops on Main Street. For starters, she still didn't know what to make of Gillian's sudden interest in West. That alone was enough to boggle her mind. But then there was Harris. For some reason he was acting completely different today. Very kind and thoughtful. Not just toward her but Grant as well. He smiled as he politely opened doors and didn't mind waiting when Grant wanted to poke around the shoe store. He was even carrying Grant's purchases.

Emma was buying gifts too. But she was trying to keep her items small enough to be tucked into carry-on bags for their trip home. She found some lovely handcrafted earrings for Mrs. Landers and Gillian, an Audubon book for Mr. Landers, and attractive handmade pens for Grant and Harris. She also bought a handsome embossed leather journal for West as a thank-you for

139

teaching her to ski. Or, if the climate between them was too much changed, she would simply keep it for herself.

Emma was standing outside, waiting for Harris and Grant to finish looking at the sporting goods shop, when she got a text from Gillian, informing Emma that she was having a great time with West. Then, without sounding overly interested, she inquired about what Emma was doing. Emma texted back about taking Grant shopping — and that Harris had come along too.

So no skiing for you guys today? Gillian texted back. But Emma made it clear that she and Harris would be there before one, suggesting they all meet up for lunch in the lodge. Gillian responded with: *Sorry, we already have plans.* Emma wanted to ask what kind of plans but was too frustrated. Well, if West and Gillian didn't want company, fine!

FOURTEEN

For several blissful minutes, West's mind felt as clear as the slope he was soaring down — with only his latest song creation playing in his head. Nothing like a good run to refresh your spirits and free up your thinking. By the time he reached the bottom, he had a plan. He texted Emma, inviting her to ski with him in the afternoon.

After about a minute, she responded. Again, it was short and terse. *Am coming to ski later.* On one hand, he felt encouraged to think he'd get to see her today. But why was she acting so chilly toward him? Maybe she wasn't into texting. He'd known a girl once who hated exchanging texts. When he'd told her he didn't have time for long phone conversations — when he'd simply had no interest — she'd taken offense and, to his relief, the relationship had withered and died. But he didn't want that to happen with Emma — and would do whatever it took to make sure it didn't.

In the meantime, he needed a graceful way to disconnect himself from Gillian. To be fair, she'd been trying hard to be Miss Congeniality, and it was possible she didn't know his real identity. Whatever the case, he needed to peel her away. There she was right now, skiing straight toward him with a bright, cheery smile.

"You should've seen me," she said happily. "I did three runs without a single stumble. And I can actually turn without using the pizza position, or snowplow, or whatever you call it. I dug in my heels the way you said to and presto — I turned. It was amazing!"

"That's great. Glad to hear it." He nodded politely.

"So I think I'm ready for a harder run."

"You sure about that?"

She frowned. "Meaning you don't think I'm ready, West?"

He shrugged. "I guess we can find out." He nodded toward the lift. "Follow me." As he got into the line, waiting for her to join him, he decided that he would use this ride to let her know that he planned to ski with Emma during the afternoon — and that this was the end of Gillian's free ski lesson. But after they got seated on the chair, Gillian initiated the conversation.

"There's something I need to tell you," she began in a serious tone.

"Oh?" He glanced at her. Was she about to confess she knew his true identity?

"It's about Emma." She looked down.

"Uh-huh?" He waited.

"Well, I didn't want to say anything, West, but it's only fair that you know. Emma is pretty much into Harris."

"Is that so?" He frowned in disbelief.

"Oh, yeah, you should've seen them on the flight to Denver. That's when the romance first took off."

"Well, you could've fooled me. Emma didn't seem the least bit interested in Harris."

"But you saw them dancing together last night," Gillian pointed out. "And how they snuck off together."

"You said Harris had a charley horse."

"Well, that's what they *said.* But it was obviously more than that."

"Obviously? Emma gave me the impression she wanted to avoid Harris."

"That's because she's been playing hard to get. You know, in order to secure his attention. It's something we both do at times. I thought she was going to use my brother, since he's always pursuing her anyway. But

143

for some reason she chose you instead. I hate to say it, but I'm pretty sure she used you to make Harris jealous."

"Is that right?" He still felt doubtful. "Used me?"

Gillian nodded. "Apparently it's working too."

"What makes you say that?"

Gillian held up her phone. "I texted her a bit ago. She and Harris are Christmas shopping together right now. Sounds like they're having a pretty great time too."

"Oh." West frowned. "She texted me that she was coming here to ski this afternoon."

"I know. But that's after they have lunch together. They probably found some romantic little spot in town. After that, they'll come here to ski *together.*"

"Oh." He slowly nodded, trying to take this in and still not fully believing it.

"Anyway, I didn't want to make you feel bad." She placed a gloved hand on his arm. "But it seems only fair that you know."

"Yeah." He nodded. "It's almost time to get off. Hope you're ready for this run, Gillian. It'll be a challenge. Take it easy." It wasn't that he wanted Gillian to fall and get hurt, but he did feel aggravated with her. If she fell on her face, he didn't expect to be overly sympathetic. It probably wasn't fair

144

to blame her for Emma being with Harris right now, but something about this whole business was suspicious.

Gillian only fell down a couple of times, and she was a good sport about it, laughing at her clumsiness. "That was fun," she said at the foot of the slope. "Should we do it again?"

"Go ahead if you want," he said. "I'm hungry. I didn't get any breakfast and it's past noon."

"You have to let me treat you to lunch. And not just fast food either. I'm taking you to a full meal at the fancy restaurant." She pointed to the lodge. "It'll be my thank-you for teaching me to ski."

"That's not necessary."

"I want to, West. The view from there must be beautiful. And I didn't have breakfast either." She pulled out her phone and did a quick search. "Here's their number. I'll call to see if we need a reservation."

Before he could stop her, she was making arrangements. Since he was ravenous, he decided to just go along with her. Maybe by the time they finished, Emma and Harris would be out here . . . and maybe he could find out what was really going on. Somehow he knew that Gillian was putting a spin on things. Emma wasn't the kind of girl to use a guy to get another one. Maybe Gillian would do that. But not Emma.

It was Grant's idea to eat at the nicest restaurant at the lodge. "That way I can linger after you guys go skiing. It'll be more comfortable there, and my cast will make a good chick magnet." Grant chuckled.

But when they got to the rather elegant restaurant, there was an hour-long wait for a table. "I'd rather grab a hot dog down-stairs and go skiing." Emma gazed longingly out the big windows of the restaurant. "The slopes are calling."

"Hey, look over there." Harris pointed across the crowded restaurant. "Gillian and West."

"Let's go eat with them," Grant said.

"The table's too small," Harris pointed out.

"But they might have room for one more," Emma told Grant. "Why don't you go crash their party?"

Grant waved to West and Gillian. "Don't mind if I do."

"Tell 'em we'll catch 'em later." Harris grabbed Emma by the hand. "We're burn-ing daylight, darling." As he tugged her out of the restaurant, she wasn't sure which was more aggravating — seeing Gil and West together like that or Harris calling her darling. Hopefully, she could forget about all of it out on the slopes.

West was about to go greet Emma and the guys, but Grant was already heading toward them. "Can you guys join us?" West asked him. "We just ordered a few minutes ago."

"Our table's not big enough," Gillian insisted before Grant could reply.

"It seats four, and we can get another chair," West countered.

"You don't need another chair." Grant sat down. "Harris and Emma decided to grab a hot dog and go skiing."

"Sounds like a good idea to me." West leaned back in his chair, wishing he could excuse himself to the slopes. "Thanks to the holidays, the restaurant is pretty busy . . . consequently pretty slow today."

"Works for me." Grant grinned.

"I'm not sure we can get the waiter back in time to place your order in time to arrive with ours," Gillian told her brother.

"That's okay. I'm in no hurry. I plan to linger."

"At the rate the waiters are moving — we'll all be lingering." West held up a finger. "I have an idea, Grant. How about if you take my order. That way you and Gillian can eat together and I'll get in some more skiing."

"Without me?" Gillian looked hurt.

"You wouldn't want to do the runs I plan to do anyway," he said.

"But Grant can't have your order, West." Gillian's smile looked triumphant. "He doesn't eat red meat, and you ordered a steak."

"That's right." Grant grimly shook his head. "Gave it up several years ago."

Seeing he was stuck, West decided to turn his attention to Grant. "I hear Harris and Emma went shopping this morning. What have you been up to?"

"I went shopping too. Actually, it was my idea. I got Emma to drive me because of this." He held up his cast. "Then Harris came along for kicks." He grinned. "He was on his best behavior. I expected him to get pushy and bossy and try to hurry us, but he was surprisingly polite."

"Obviously, that was for Emma's sake," Gillian said.

"I don't think so. I give credit to that hard ski run West took him on yesterday. It seems to have softened old Harris up a bit." He winked at West. "Nice work, man."

"Well, if Harris softened up, it has more to do with Emma than West," Gillian told

148

her brother. "You know as well as anyone that Harris is over the moon for her. And if you ask me, he's a pretty good catch for Emma. He's got money and looks and a great family. Emma would be well set with him."

"You sound pretty sure of yourself." West studied her, trying to decide if she was devious, deluded, or delirious . . . maybe all three.

"That's because I've known Emma and Harris for years," she told him. "I wouldn't be surprised if Harris pops the question by Christmas. Wouldn't it be romantic if Emma and Harris got engaged during the holidays?"

"Seriously?" Grant frowned. "You honestly think Emma likes Harris *that much*?"

"You must be blind if you can't see it. But you weren't with us last night. You should've seen those two slow dancing. Then they left early. And leaving the rest of us behind just now — to run off to ski together. Seriously, the writing is on the wall, Grant." She patted his shoulder. "Sorry, bro. But as they say, there are lots more fish in the sea."

West grimaced at her mixed metaphors, but Grant looked seriously dismayed.

"Yeah . . . you're probably right." Grant glumly shook his head. "I should've known

149

Emma was way out of my league."

"Don't feel bad, Grant. You're just not her type. I've been telling you that for years. But you've got a lot to offer — when you find a girl who appreciates you." She tapped his cast. "And with that, you'll be sure to attract some sympathetic chicks this afternoon. Just sit by yourself next to the big fireplace with a lonely expression and a hot drink, and they'll be eating out of your hand."

"You think so?"

"Sure. It worked for me — and I didn't even have an injury."

West felt his phone buzz and realized his mom had probably just left a voice mail. "Excuse me, I need to get back to my family about Christmas plans." Before Gillian could say another word, he hurried to the lobby, calling his mother.

"How's it going?" she asked eagerly. "Making progress with the girl? By the way, what's her name, West? And what does she look like? Is she part of the family who live here —"

"Really? Is that why you called, Mom? To play twenty questions?" Now he regretted calling her back.

"You sound a little grumpy, West. Is everything okay?"

150

"I'm not sure."

"I'm sorry. I shouldn't have pounded you with questions. I suppose I'm curious."

"Well, I'll answer one question. The girl's name is Emma."

"Emma. That's pretty."

"And she is too."

"Then why do you sound unhappy? What's going on there?"

He told her about his day so far. "It's pretty frustrating. I keep getting stuck with the wrong girl. This Gillian chick is Emma's friend, but those girls are as different as night and day. I just can't seem to peel Gillian off. Seriously, she's like flypaper."

"That doesn't sound good."

"Just because I gave Gillian a little ski lesson, she acts like we're a couple. And she totally refuses to take a hint." He explained about Gillian buying him lunch. "So I stupidly ordered the most expensive steak. But now I don't want to go back in there. Except that I'm pretty hungry."

"Well, go back and enjoy your steak. But after you're done, you just politely thank Miss Flypaper then give her the gentle brush-off and go your own way."

"You make it sound so easy, Mom."

She laughed. "It is easy. Like the shoe ad. *Just do it.*"

He peered back into the restaurant to see if their food had been served, but it appeared the waiter was taking Grant's order now. "I'll try to."

"Anyway, West, I'm sure you'll be glad to hear that your nephews just started to complain about not being at your house for Christmas — they want to go skiing."

He chuckled. "I figured as much."

"And it's too hot for me here. I mostly stay inside. To be honest, I think the charm of a warm desert Christmas is wearing thin on everyone."

"Even your husband?"

She gave a little groan. "I think Drew is having regrets too, but he keeps acting like it's all just wonderful."

"And you're playing along?" West knew his mom well enough to know she was.

"Well, I don't want to spoil it for anyone. Between you and me, I wish I were there with you. I'd love to meet your girl. Hey, do you have any pictures on your phone — something you can send me?"

"No . . . but I'll try to take some. If I can ever get her away from Harris."

"Harris? Is that Gillian's brother?"

"No. It's complicated, Mom. I *thought* Harris was Gillian's boyfriend at first. But now Gillian's trying to make me her boyfriend — well, it's a big old mess."

"I bet that Gillian girl figured out who you are, West. Do you think it's possible she found out you're not actually the caretaker?"

"I'm suspicious. But she acts clueless." He peeked into the restaurant again. "Looks like food is coming to our table, Mom. I better go."

As he hung up and headed back to the table, he replayed his mom's advice to give Gillian the gentle brush-off. Hadn't he been trying to do that already? Without success? Maybe he should leave the gentle part off.

West devoured his steak so quickly that he hoped his stomach could handle it. Wiping his mouth with a napkin, he briskly thanked Gillian. "Now if you'll both excuse me, I plan to get in some serious runs. Take your time here, and I'll catch up with you guys later." He grinned at Grant. "Good luck playing Mr. Snow Bunny." Although Gillian looked miffed, West just left. This would be the beginning of the brush-off. His only goal for the remaining afternoon was to cross paths with Emma.

When he got outside, he texted Emma, asking where she was at and if she wanted to ski with him. When he got no answer, he decided to go looking. After standing at the bottom of the bunny hill for twenty minutes, he decided she had to be skiing a different run. He checked out the lines at the nearby mid-level runs, waiting long enough for skiers to go up and come down, and still didn't see her.

Not wanting to feel dishonest, he went over to the nearest black diamond chairlift and after a short wait in line, went up. He knew he wouldn't see Emma and Harris up here . . . but maybe that was for the best. He could use some head-clearing time.

FIFTEEN

When Harris recommended they try some new ski runs, Emma wasn't sure. But when he showed her the map, explaining these intermediate runs were easier than the crowded one they'd been using, Emma agreed. She was surprised that they had to be shuttled to another part of the mountain. Still, he was right, the runs were easier — and they were longer too. Plus the lift lines were shorter.

"I really like it over here," she told Harris after they finished a run that had only tripped her up once. "But my phone doesn't get any bars."

"And my phone is dead."

"I'm a little concerned about Grant. With his bad arm and shopping all morning, he might be worn out by now. What if he wants to go home?"

"West can give him a ride. After all, he's the caretaker, so he should take care of the

155

houseguests, right?" Harris's eyes twinkled.

"Maybe . . . but we're the ones who brought Grant up here. So I feel sort of responsible."

"How about we do one more run here and then go back and check on him?"

"That sounds good."

By the time they got back to the lodge where Grant had planned to sip cocoa and garner female sympathy, they couldn't find him anywhere. When he finally responded to Emma's text, he said he was on his way home with West and Gillian. There was also a short text from West, sent a couple hours ago, inviting her to ski with him — or them — but she suspected it had simply been a pity invite and would most likely include skiing with Gillian too. She was glad to have missed it.

"Sounds like the others went home already," she told Harris. "I'm ready to call it quits too. Do you mind?"

"Not at all. I'm still a little sore from yesterday."

As Harris drove them toward town, Emma's phone pinged with a text from Gillian. "Interesting . . ." She read it then set her phone down with a long sigh.

"What's that?" he asked.

"Gillian is fixing dinner tonight."

"You're kidding. I didn't think she could cook."

"You and me both. Anyway, she wants us to stop by the store for a few things."

He laughed. "I never took old Gillian for the domestic type. But then I didn't think she'd ever try skiing. That girl's just full of surprises."

"Yeah." Emma felt very close to tears as they came into town. What had looked so incredibly beautiful last night seemed to hurt her eyes now. She tried to tell herself she was simply tired . . . or perhaps home-sick for her parents. But the truth was this was all about West. She knew it was silly to feel so emotional about a guy she'd only known a couple of days. And yet everything about West had felt so amazingly magical. But then, just like a magic trick, it had vanished right before her eyes. Thanks to Gillian.

"You're being awfully quiet," Harris said.

"Just thinking."

"So what do you think about Gillian and the caretaker?" he asked.

She turned to stare at him — *was he clairvoyant?* "Well, to be honest, it's been pretty mind-boggling."

"I know." He nodded. "I actually thought Gil was using West to make me jealous."

"That occurred to me too." Unfortunately, Gillian had only managed to make Emma jealous. Not that she planned to admit as much to Harris — or anyone. "But it seems like there's more to it. I'm guessing Gillian's sudden domesticity is for West's benefit. I'll bet she invited him to dinner tonight."

"You're probably right. But I still don't get it. Everyone knows Gillian's a climber . . . she's like the ultimate material girl. So why is she suddenly so smitten with our lowly caretaker? I mean, West is a nice guy and not bad looking. But — give me a break — he's a *ski bum.*"

Emma had to bite her tongue to keep from defending West. Sure, maybe he was a caretaker and maybe even a ski bum, but she didn't like hearing Harris talk down about him. Still, she didn't want to argue with Harris — not when she was this close to tears.

"Just drop me by the front door of the store," she said as he entered the packed parking lot. "I should be able to get everything on Gil's list in about fifteen minutes or so. I'll text you when I've checked out and you can just drive by and pick me up here."

Based on Gillian's list of ingredients, fettuccini alfredo, green salad, French bread, and "some good dessert" were on tonight's menu. Even though Gillian didn't actually cook, anyone could easily make this entrée with the fresh pasta and canned alfredo sauce Emma put into the basket. For a brief moment, Emma was tempted to get the real ingredients and offer to make dinner from scratch, but she knew Gillian would probably throw a fit. Or else, she'd pretend like she'd made it herself in order to impress West. And Emma just wasn't going there. As bamboozling as this whole thing was, she knew Gil had something up her sleeve. For some reason, she was into West. The question was — why? Was it competition? She wanted to take him from Emma? Or maybe she thought she was protecting Emma. It wouldn't be the first time. Or maybe she just wanted a little holiday fling . . . with a "ski bum." Who could know?

But Emma knew one thing as she gathered Gillian's items. She would not be dining with the others tonight. Emma would claim a headache — which she felt truly coming on. She'd take some food up to her room and just call it a night. Maybe she'd remain up in her room throughout Christmas as well. Or maybe she would get an earlier flight and simply go home to Arizona tomorrow. Anything to avoid having to be around West . . . and Gillian . . . and whatever games they were playing.

The only reason West had agreed to have dinner with the Landerses and their house-guests tonight was because it would give him an opportunity to see Emma. After not finding her on the slopes today — and the way she'd ignored his text — he was desperate to talk to her. He had to find out what had gone wrong . . . and somehow he had to fix it. He felt so desperate to figure this out that he'd even taken Grant into his confidence.

"I know your sister's convinced that Emma's into Harris," he told Grant while Gillian was upstairs getting cleaned up. "But I find it pretty hard to believe."

"Me too." Grant nodded. "I mean, I understand why Harris likes Emma. Who doesn't like Emma? But she's always kind of held him at arm's length. Even more than she does me. But I think that's because she sees me more like a brother." His smile seemed halfhearted. "And I guess that's okay. Emma makes a pretty good sister."

"Yeah. I can see that." West ran his fingers through his messy hair. "But I really want to talk to Emma — alone, you know?"

"You mean without Gillian's interference."

"Exactly. But that might not be easy."

"So you need sort of a wingman?" Grant's brows arched.

"Yeah. I could use a wingman. You interested?"

"Sure. Might be fun."

"And if it turns out that Emma actually likes Harris, well, I'll just bow out gracefully. In fact, I'll probably just go spend Christmas with my family."

"Don't blame you for that, man." Grant rubbed his chin. "So here's a plan. How about if I arrange for you to meet with Emma alone — *before* dinner."

"Sounds good."

"Gillian said dinner's at seven, so how about you come over early — like six-thirty? I'll keep Gil occupied, and you can talk to Emma."

"Great. And here's a heads-up. If I make a hasty exit before dinner — you can let your family know the caretaker has taken the holidays off."

"Meaning Emma will have given you your walking papers?"

"Yeah, something like that."

"Aw, that won't happen."

As West headed to his studio, he wasn't so

sure. He even considered calling the airlines for a standby red-eye flight to Phoenix. He could make the drive to Denver tonight and surprise his family early tomorrow morning — Christmas Eve. Sure, Arizona might not feel much like Christmas, but it would be better than holing up in his studio or having to witness the budding romance between Emma and Harris. If Gillian's prediction was right and they really did get engaged on Christmas — West wasn't sure he could take it.

But he wasn't ready to throw in the towel just yet. Before he gave up on Emma completely, he had to speak to her — *alone.* First he needed a good long shower and a change of clothes. Then he needed some sort of plan.

Emma and Harris carried the grocery bags into the kitchen only to find it dark and quiet with no one around. "What time is this dinner party taking place?" Harris asked her as they put things away.

"I don't know, and I don't particularly care since I'm not planning to come." She took a yogurt, apple, and bagel and set them on a plate. "I'll dine in my room tonight."

"No, you won't." Grant popped into the kitchen, holding up his cast-enclosed arm

162

like a stop sign. "Sit down, Emma."

"Huh?" She stared at him.

"I need to talk to you. *Alone.*"

She blinked then exchanged glances with Harris, but he just chuckled and, after grabbing something to snack on, excused himself to go clean up. "Let me know if you two are planning to elope or something," he called over his shoulder.

"Very funny," Grant shot back at him.

"What's going on?" Emma sat down on a stool by the island and waited.

"Here's the deal, Emma. West needs you to be here tonight. He wants to talk to you."

"Oh?" She took a bite of the apple, feigning nonchalance.

"Yeah. And I happen to know Gil wants this to be a romantic dinner for two. She already insisted Dad take Mom out tonight. And she wants me to take you and Harris out as well. She even made a reservation for the three of us. That way it'll be just her and West."

"Cozy." Emma took another bite, slowly chewing.

"That's how she wants it — cozy . . . just the two of them."

"Well, you can go out with Harris if you want, Grant, but I'm not going anywhere tonight."

"Then you'll eat dinner down here with them?"

She firmly shook her head. "Like I said, I'm going to my room."

"But West is only coming tonight in order to see you. So you can't hide out in your room."

"What do you suggest I do? Crash a candlelit dinner for two? Sit there and watch Gillian flirting with West? Act like it's all just peachy keen and I don't care?"

"So you *do* have feelings for West?"

"I didn't say that, Grant. I just said I don't want to —"

"What if we all crash Gil's dinner?" he said. "You and me and Harris. Dinner for five. That way I can distract Gil long enough for you and West to have a conversation."

"You're overlooking one little thing, Grant." She stood.

"What's that?"

"What if West does have feelings for Gillian?"

"He doesn't. I *know* he doesn't." Grant leaned over the island, looking squarely into her eyes. "I always think of you as a gutsy girl. Are you seriously going to just step aside and let Gillian run this circus? Meanwhile you hide out in your room and don't lift a finger. Don't put up a fight?"

"Fight? Seriously?" She frowned.

"If you like West as much as he seems to like you, you should be willing to put some effort into this, Emma Daley."

She pursed her lips. "Yeah . . . I suppose you're right."

"I mean, West might just be a caretaker, but he's a good guy. And he really likes you — and I know you really like him." Grant scratched his head. "What I can't figure out is my sister. She's the wild card here."

"Okay, you talked me into it, Grant. If you and Harris promise to stay for dinner, I will too." Emma picked up her plate. "But since Gillian's cooking, I'm going to eat this first."

"Good idea. I better grab something too. Gillian told West seven, but he's coming at six-thirty. I'll text you when he gets here."

Emma patted his shoulder. "Thanks, Grant. You make a very decent brother."

"Maybe to you, but I doubt Gillian will think so after tonight."

Emma chuckled on her way upstairs. She appreciated Grant's help and interest, but she wasn't sure how Gillian would react. Still, something was up with Gillian . . . something that Emma wanted to figure out. Deep inside, Emma knew that Gillian couldn't possibly have sincere interest in a caretaker. Good grief, he probably made less than Emma did as a substitute teacher. And Gillian loved money and things, leisure and prestige. She'd never made it a secret that she planned to marry a millionaire. The whole biz just did not compute.

But if Gillian was using West — either to make Harris jealous or simply for her own egotistical pleasure — it was just plain wrong. And Grant was absolutely right, Emma should put up a fight. She just hoped West wouldn't get hurt in the process. For all she knew, he might've gotten caught up in Gillian's game. Because Emma knew it was a game. But what was the prize?

SIXTEEN

West had a plan. When he went over to the main house at half past six, he was ready to execute it. Dressed as well as he could manage with the clothing he'd sneaked from his own closet in the master suite, he was also armed — with a guitar. Grant opened the door before West even knocked.

"Gillian's in the kitchen," he whispered. "Up to her elbows in pasta."

"And Emma?"

"I'll text her to come down and meet you. How about the den?"

"Good idea."

Grant pointed to the guitar case. "What's that for? Planning to woo her with song?"

"You never know."

Grant nodded. "Well, nice touch, man."

West quietly went into the den, closed the heavy door, and sat down to wait. Not for the first time today, he said a silent prayer that this thing would turn out the way it was meant to be — and for the best for both of them.

"Here you are." Grant opened the door, and Emma, looking more beautiful than West remembered, came into the room. She had on a silky emerald top, jeans, and boots, but it was those dark brown eyes, her sleek dark hair . . . and the shy smile that made his heart beat a little faster.

"I'll go keep sis occupied until dinnertime," Grant told them.

"I'm sure she could use a hand," Emma said quietly.

After Grant left, they both sat down and West thanked her for coming — trying to remember what he wanted to say but feeling distracted by her beauty.

"This is one of my favorite rooms in the house," he began nervously.

"I like it." She sounded uneasy too.

"So . . . anyway, I asked Grant to help us get together so that we could talk . . . without Gillian's interference."

"Right." She seemed to be studying him.

"For, uh, some mysterious reason, Gillian seems to have set her sights on me. And no matter what I say or do, I can't seem to shake her off."

"Gillian can be pretty determined sometimes." She tilted her head to one side.

168

"So I've noticed. That woman is a force to be reckoned with."

"Especially when she really wants something."

"Tell me about it."

"Gillian is sort of used to getting her own way. Her dad says he spoiled her too much . . . maybe that's true."

"So, anyway, I wanted to make sure you hadn't gotten the wrong idea about me . . . I mean, where Gillian's concerned. I have absolutely no interest in her. Zero. Nada. Nothing."

Emma still looked slightly doubtful. "You've sure been spending a lot of time with her."

"A lot more time than I wanted to spend. I've seen some schemers before, Emma, but nothing like Gillian." He explained how she'd entrapped him in a number of situations. "I'm also discovering how much she twists the truth. She made me believe you and Harris were, well, involved. She said you two went Christmas shopping together — I mean, just the two of you, like a date. But then Grant told me it was his idea to go, and that all three of you went."

"That's true."

"Grant doesn't seem to think you're interested in Harris. Not like Gillian wants me to believe. Only today, she predicted that you and Harris would be engaged by Christmas."

"That's ridiculous." She looked down at her lap.

"Well, if you have any feelings for him, I'd like to know, Emma. Then I'll just wish you both the best and get out of the way."

She looked up, directly into his eyes. "Grant got it right, West. Harris is only a friend, and that's all he'll ever be."

He let out a sigh. "That's good to know."

"And I have no idea why Gil would want you to think otherwise. Well, except that she seems to want you all to herself."

"Exactly." He nodded.

"Which is pretty puzzling."

"Believe me, I know. But I'm glad we got this all out into the open, Emma. What a relief."

"It does feel good to clear the air." She smiled.

Suddenly they were both talking, asking questions, trying to fit the confusing pieces of the last twenty-four hours together, and finally laughing over how they'd both been duped by Gillian. Then the door to the den flew open.

"I thought I heard voices in here." Gillian, looking less glamorous than usual, frowned at Emma. "Grant says you're staying for dinner. You and Harris and Grant. I thought the three of you were going out tonight."

"What made you think that?" Emma asked innocently.

"Because you guys have reservations at —"

"The reservations you made?" Emma frowned. "Well, Grant didn't want to go — and neither did I. Are you worried there's not enough food, Gil? Because when I did your grocery shopping, I assumed you were cooking for seven — so there should be plenty for just the five of us. But if you don't want me there, I'm happy to take something up to my room and —"

"Or I can take Emma out," West interrupted. "That should leave plenty for the rest of you."

"Oh, never mind — no biggie." Gillian's smile looked forced. "But if you're staying for dinner, Em, seems like you could help."

"I can help too." West stood.

"Thank you, West." Gillian's smile grew even sweeter. "Could you, please, make us a fire? I think that would be so cozy."

"You got it." He nodded. "And I'll make one in the fire pit out back too."

"Oh, that's okay. We won't need to go outside —"

"But I want to make one," he said. "It's a clear, starry night. Perfect for an outdoor fire."

"Oh, that sounds fun," Emma told him.

"Sounds cold to me." Gillian grabbed Emma's hand. "Come on, girlfriend. I haven't even started the salad yet."

West felt the spring return to his step as he built the fires — both inside and out. Then he went ahead and cleared snow off the back patio and benches and even set out some fleecy blankets. Unless he was mistaken, he still had ingredients for s'mores left over from Thanksgiving. This could turn into a pretty cool evening. And with Gillian's unpredictable antics — that he and Emma were now prepared for — it might even be entertaining.

It was clear that Gillian needed help in the kitchen, so Emma jumped right in. First she suggested Gillian go set the table, and then she rescued the pasta that Gillian had left standing in a pan of water. Cold water.

"How's it going?" Grant asked quietly as he peeked into the kitchen.

"Just fine." She smiled. "Hey, thanks for your help with West."

"Why did you get stuck on KP? This is supposed to be Gillian's gig."

"Because I thought it would be nice if our dinner was edible." She winked and he laughed.

By the time Gillian returned, Emma was working on the green salad.

"So what were you and West talking about in the den?" Gillian asked. "What was so funny?"

"Oh, just this and that. Lots of random things." Emma chopped the green onions with more vigor. She did not want to go there with Gillian right now.

"Well, it seems you've got it under control in here." Gillian patted her hair. "I'm going to freshen up and then spend some time with West."

"Well, everything should be ready in about fifteen minutes." Emma chopped even harder. It wasn't that she was concerned for West's sake. But how could Gillian honestly continue to assume he was interested in her? She couldn't be that oblivious . . . could she? Ironic since she liked to tease Emma for gullibility.

When the salad was finished and the sauce and pasta were hot, Emma started to slice the loaf of bread then decided she'd done enough. This was Gillian's dinner party. Let her do something to help. Emma laid down the knife and went out to discover Gillian, now wearing a fuzzy pink sweater, standing in front of the Christmas tree, dramatically telling the three guys about how she'd nearly mowed down a small pack of preteen snowboarders today.

"You should've heard their filthy little mouths." Gillian shook her fist. "If I was their mom, I'd wash their tongues with soap."

"Sorry to interrupt." Emma tapped Gillian on the shoulder. "But everything's almost ready for dinner."

"And you put it on the table?"

"I wasn't sure how you planned to serve it, Gil. I mean, you're the hostess." Emma sat down on the sofa, crossing one leg over the other — and feeling stubborn.

Gillian frowned then turned to her brother. "Why don't you help me?"

"I'm crippled." He pointed to his cast.

"And you're the hostess," Harris parroted Emma.

"And West is in charge of the fire," Emma said before Gil had a chance to drag him away. "It looks like it needs more wood."

"Real nice, people." Gillian narrowed her eyes at Emma. "Thanks a lot."

"Hey, Emma already did most of the work," Grant pointed out.

"And the grocery shopping," Harris added.

"I might as well help her." Emma reluctantly stood. "That is if we want to eat tonight."

"I'm ever so grateful," Gillian said with sarcasm.

When they got to the kitchen, Emma handed Gillian the bread knife then wondered if that was terribly wise considering Gil's current disposition. "Uh, why don't you slice the bread while I dish up the pasta?"

Gillian cut into the loaf. "I just don't know why you're being so mean to me, Emma."

"Mean?"

"Yeah, it's like you've turned on me or something."

"I've turned on *you*?" Emma paused from dishing pasta into the serving bowl. "I thought it was the other way around."

"You mean because of West?" Gillian turned to look at her with innocent-looking blue eyes. "Are you jealous because of that? Because I can't help it if West likes me better than you."

Emma slid the rest of the pasta into the bowl, trying to think of an appropriate response . . . without starting a regrettable fight. "Do you honestly believe West likes you better than me?"

"It seems obvious. We've been spending all our time together lately. And I don't see why you should care since you've been spending all your time with Harris."

"Not intentionally." Emma poured the alfredo sauce over the pasta. "Although it seems you've been pretty intentional about spending time with West."

"Sure, why not?"

"Well, how about the fact that you barely tolerated him at first — because he's a caretaker. Remember?"

"I'll admit I was acting pretty snooty. And that was wrong."

"Yeah, but that still doesn't explain your sudden interest in *the caretaker.*"

"Ooh, Em, now you sound like a snob." She laughed.

Instead of responding, Emma focused on stirring the pasta.

"Surely, you've heard opposites attract, Em. And wouldn't you agree that West and I are almost total and complete opposites?"

"Yeah, I'd agree with that. But you must know that West isn't the guy for you, Gil. You're not dumb."

"What do you mean by that?" Gillian stopped slicing bread.

"I mean, anyone can see that he's not really into you." Emma poured dressing over the salad then gave it a good toss.

"Oh, Emma, don't you think that's between West and me?" She shook her knife. "And FYI, he and I would've been having a nice, intimate dinner tonight if you and the guys hadn't invited yourselves to crash our little party."

"Gillian." Emma moved closer, looking into her friend's face. "You can't possibly be this oblivious. Don't you know that West doesn't really like you? Not like *that* anyway. Not how you seem to like him. Sure, he's polite to you — because he's a nice guy. But he's *not* into you."

"What gives you the right to speak for West?" Gillian sounded angry.

Emma held up her hands. "Nothing. You're right. West can speak for himself. But I'm your friend, Gil, and I don't want to see you get hurt."

"I don't plan on getting hurt."

"Right . . . but honestly I don't know why you're doing this. I mean, can you honestly say that you care that much for West? Or is this some kind of game for you? Because none of it makes sense. Not to any of us. Harris and Grant both think you've lost your mind. And I thought maybe you were competing with me — or maybe even trying to protect me." Emma peered closely at her. "Are you?"

Gillian's grin looked victorious. "Not this time, girlfriend. This is about me. Me and West."

"So you're saying you have genuine feelings for West? You're that serious about him?"

"Maybe." Gillian returned to slicing bread.

Emma sighed as she carried the salad and pasta bowls to the dining table. This was not going to be easy. But maybe it was time for West to step in and straighten Gil out. Hopefully not until after dinner.

"Hey, West," Gillian called out sweetly as she brought out the bread basket. "Since you're in charge of the fire, how about lighting these candles for me?"

"At your service." He appeared with the lighter.

"Come and get it," she called out. "If you guys have any complaints, aim them at Emma. Compliments can come to me." She laughed as they all sat down.

Emma couldn't help but be impressed with how easily Gillian played the role of hostess, even being polite to Emma, as if they hadn't just had that awkward conversa-

178

tion in the kitchen. As a result, Emma's stomach was tied in knots and she mostly just poked at her food.

"Compliments to the cooks," Harris said as he set down his fork. "That was good pasta."

"To be fair, it should probably be compliments to the grocery store and food packagers," Emma confessed. "We just put it together."

"Well, the salad was great," West said. "Looks like some thought and effort went into that. In fact, it's all been good."

"Thank you, West." Gillian beamed at him. "I'm glad you like it. And there's still dessert."

"I have another plan for dessert." He grinned. "We'll have it outside. Around the fire pit. Along with some music, if Emma doesn't object to playing for us."

"I never object to music." She stood to gather empty plates.

"Let Gillian take care of that," West told her. "I need you to help me."

"Okay." She set the plates by Gil and followed him back to the den.

"Here." He handed her the guitar case. "I meant to give you this earlier, but we were interrupted."

"Huh?" She stared at the case. "Oh, yeah,

179

you promised to loan me your guitar. Thanks."

"This isn't a loan, Emma."

"What do you mean?" She looked at him, seeing a twinkle in his eyes, like he was amused.

"It's a gift. Call it an early Christmas present if you like."

"You can't be serious."

"I am. Open it."

She laid the hard case on the desk and slowly opened it. "Oh, West. It's so beautiful." She picked it up to examine the guitar more closely. "It's a Martin, isn't it?"

He nodded. "Yep."

"But it's way too nice. You can't give me this."

"I can if I want."

"But it had to be expensive." She knew a guitar like this could run close to five grand. How could he afford it?

"You're not supposed to question a gift, Emma. Bad manners."

"But — I —"

"I *want* you to have it. And I want you to play it tonight. We can jam together out by the fire. It'll be fun."

"What will you play?"

He went over to the big wooden cabinet that filled one wall. He unlocked and opened it to reveal a number of beautiful instruments inside — banjo, mandolin, ukulele, and a couple more guitars. He removed a handsome guitar. "This'll work."

"Isn't that your boss's guitar?" She felt seriously worried. This guitar looked even more valuable than the one he'd just presented to her.

"It does belong to the homeowner . . ." He paused to tune it.

"But aren't you stepping over the line, West? Won't you get in trouble?"

"Nah, he's pretty understanding." He grinned like this was fun. "Let's grab some coats and get outside before the others. We can warm up a little." He led her through the mudroom, where he helped her into a long fleecy coat.

"You're sure it's okay to use this?" She frowned.

"Sure. These spares are for guests." Now he got out a wooden box filled with graham crackers, marshmallows, and chocolate bars. "For dessert."

"Sounds good." She nodded, but still felt worried. West was taking too many liberties with his boss's generosity. What if he got fired? But before long, they were out by the fire pit, and as West stoked it up with more wood, she pushed her worries aside and

181

began to play the gorgeous guitar. It sounded great.

"You're not half bad." He grinned.

"It's the guitar. It sounds fabulous." She smiled back at him but still felt concerned. How could he afford to give her such a fine instrument? What if it, like the one he was using, actually belonged to the house? She couldn't believe West was deceitful or a thief, and she hated to keep questioning him about this. Especially since he seemed so happy tonight. He was clearly in his element — and a surprisingly good musician.

"You're really good," she said after they finished a familiar folk song.

"You sound surprised." He chuckled as he broke into a Gunner Price song — one that she loved and knew by heart. As they played it together, taking turns on the vocals, Emma couldn't believe how well their voices blended. When the song ended, his expression turned serious. "Emma, there's something I need to tell —"

"Hey, that last song sounded great," Harris called out. He and Grant, dressed warmly, came over to the fire.

"Yeah. You guys could seriously go pro," Grant added.

They thanked them, and West started another Gunner Price song. One that Emma knew well enough to sing harmony throughout. While Harris and Grant roasted marshmallows, they joined in on the chorus. The four of them didn't sound too bad.

In the midst of another robust tune, Gillian came outside, followed by her parents. Mr. and Mrs. Landers seemed pleased about the impromptu music fest, but Emma could tell by Gillian's scowl she was in a bad mood.

"What a great idea." Mr. Landers reached for a marshmallow roasting stick. "Music and s'mores. It's like being at sleepover camp."

"How about some Christmas songs?" Mrs. Landers suggested.

So West and Emma did some fun, singalong Christmas songs like "The Twelve Days of Christmas" and "Rudolph." Everyone was happily singing, roasting marshmallows, and eating s'mores — everyone except for Gillian. Her expression had turned even more sour, and between songs, she complained about the cold.

"You certainly do make yourself at home here," Mrs. Landers said to West as he threw another log on the fire. "I hope your boss doesn't mind."

"Oh, his boss doesn't mind." Gillian's tone suddenly turned sly.

"How would *you* know?" Grant held his marshmallow stick in front of her.

"I have my ways." She grabbed off his gooey marshmallow and popped it into her mouth with a smirk.

"Thanks a lot." Grant shook the stick at her.

"Have you even *met* his boss?" Harris challenged Gillian.

"Sure." She licked her fingers, narrowing her eyes at West. "Haven't I?"

"How could you possibly meet West's boss?" her dad questioned. "He and his family are spending Christmas at our place in Scottsdale right now and —"

"Oh, his family might be at our house, but he didn't go," she said glibly.

Emma glanced at West to see he looked perplexed — or was it embarrassed? Perhaps he felt worried to think his boss might still be around. But how did Gillian know so much about this? What was going on here?

"So where'd you meet West's boss?" Harris pressed Gillian. "Here in Breckenridge? Does he own other properties? And what's he do for a living anyway? The dude's got to be pretty rich."

"Oh, yeah. He's very rich. But he's also very dishonest."

"How do you know so much about him?"

her mother demanded.

"Because I spent a lot of time with him."

"When?" Grant asked her.

West loudly cleared his throat. "I think it's time I did some explaining."

"Please, do. If you can." Mr. Landers sounded seriously aggravated.

"Yeah, this should be good." Gillian chuckled.

"This is my house," West said solemnly.

"You mean because you're the caretaker," Mrs. Landers clarified. "It might feel like your house, but I'm sure your boss wouldn't agree —"

"I *am* the boss," West admitted. "I own this house."

"How is that even possible?" Harris demanded. "You'd have to be —"

"He's TW Prescott," Gillian declared triumphantly. "You've all heard of Gunner Price since his music is everywhere. He even played it tonight. So get this, gang, West's full name is *Tyler West Prescott,* aka TW Prescott. And he's made literally millions as the creator of most of Gunner Price's biggest hits. He also writes songs for other well-known musicians." She wrapped an arm around West's shoulders, like they had some special bond or unspoken understanding. "Our buddy West here has been going incognito as the caretaker. And also as our rather popular ski instructor. And, just for the record, the so-called caretaker's cottage is actually his music studio. Right, West?" She grinned at him.

He simply nodded, and suddenly they were all asking him questions, slapping him on the back, shaking his hand, and treating him like a real celebrity. Everyone except Emma. Feeling totally blindsided, she quietly set down the expensive guitar, and as Mr. Landers quizzed West about why he'd remained here instead of going to Arizona, Emma slipped back into the house and went upstairs.

All this time, West had been pretending to be someone he wasn't? Who does that? And why? Even more irritating — and just like the gullible girl Gillian always claimed her to be — Emma had swallowed it whole. Hook, line, and sinker. She'd even gone as far as to imagine the simple sort of life she and West might enjoy together someday. She'd dreamed of something not so very different from her parents' relationship. Except that, besides the need to work for a living, she and West would have their music to enrich their unpretentious lives. And they would have true love to sustain them.

It had been a pretty picture. But that sweet

186

scene had been blasted to smithereens when Gillian made her startling announcement. Now Emma didn't know what to think. She felt like the brunt of a bad joke . . . like she'd been tricked . . . humiliated. All she wanted now was to escape.

SEVENTEEN

By the time West realized Emma had disappeared — without taking the guitar he'd given her — it was pretty late. He excused himself from his new fan club, saying he was ready to call it a night. He put away the guitars and extinguished the fire, but before going inside for the night, he peered up to the third floor to see that the master suite window was darkened. She must've already gone to bed.

Back in his studio, West started to pace. He knew he'd created a big fat mess where Emma was concerned. What a way for her to discover his true identity. To have Gillian announce it like that to everyone — and she'd obviously done her research — poor Emma had probably gotten the wrong idea. Besides feeling deceived, she probably now assumed that Gillian, with the inside track, had to be more involved than West had told her. Somehow, he had to straighten it out.

He picked up his phone but didn't want to wake her. He considered sending a text, but that was impersonal. He knew it was best to wait until morning. He also knew that his feelings for Emma were far deeper than he'd realized before. Just the thought of hurting her . . . losing her . . . was excruciating. Emma was the one. He felt certain of it. So West did what he did best, he sat down and wrote the lyrics to a new song. A song for Emma. Then, in the wee hours of the morning, he finally went to bed.

West woke up to the sound of someone knocking on his door. Realizing he'd slept late, he hurried to open it — hoping it was Emma. But it was Gillian. He tried not to growl at her.

"Have you seen Emma?" she asked.

He frowned. "Not since last night. Why?"

Gillian bit her lip. "She's gone."

"Gone?" He checked the clock to see it was nine. "Maybe she went skiing. The lifts are open —"

"No. All her things are gone. She packed and left."

"*She left?* How? When? Did she take the car?"

"No. My dad thinks she might've called for a taxi. He heard a vehicle in the driveway early this morning. We thought you might

189

know something."

"No." He ran his fingers through his hair. "She didn't text you or leave a note or anything?"

"No. And I tried to call, but her phone goes straight to voice mail."

"Where do you think she went?"

"Probably home." Gillian sighed. "And it's most likely my fault."

West wanted to agree with that, but since she already looked troubled, he decided to keep his thoughts to himself. "Then she's probably on her way to the airport. That might explain her phone not working. There are dead spots through the mountains."

"Do you think she could get a flight out of Denver? I mean, it is Christmas Eve. Seems like flights would be booked full."

"Yeah, but you never know."

"Well, sorry to bother you about this." Gillian stepped back.

"No, I'm glad you did. I mean, I'm sad Emma's gone, but it's good to know."

"And . . . I should apologize. I'm sorry for outing you like that last night."

"Yeah, that was pretty awkward. Hey, before you leave, can you give me Emma's address?"

"You mean her house address in Tempe?"

"Yeah." He grabbed his phone. "Where

does she live?"

"Why? Are you going to write her a letter?"

"No. I'm going to go there."

"Seriously?" Gillian blinked. "You've got it bad for her, huh?"

"Bad." He nodded somberly. "What airline did you and your family fly out with — do you think she'll take it home?"

After getting the information, he thanked her. "I plan to leave ASAP. But if you hear from her, could you shoot me a text?"

"Yeah. And you do the same." Her brow creased. "I know I wasn't being a very good friend to her . . . and Emma's really sweet. She deserves better."

He nodded. "Yep. She sure does. I'll let you know if I catch up with her."

"Well, uh, merry Christmas."

"Yeah, back at you." He closed the door, then scrambled to get himself together. Fortunately his bags for Arizona were still packed.

Before he left, he remembered something. Slipping into the back door of the house, he heard voices out in the great room speculating about Emma's hasty departure. Using the back staircase, he went up to the master suite.

Everything in his room looked just like

191

he'd left it — before his house swap guests had arrived — but he could still feel Emma's presence there and, unless he imagined it, he even got a whiff of something sweet in the air. He unlocked his closet and, after a brief search, found what he was looking for. He wrapped it in an old blue bandana and slipped it into his jeans pocket. Then, slipping back down unnoticed, he went outside and got into his Jeep.

West wasn't anxious to spend Christmas in Arizona, but if it allowed him to be with Emma, he would gladly spend Christmas anywhere — the North Pole or Tahiti. All he wanted was to find her again. And wouldn't his family be thrilled to have him show up unexpectedly — with Emma on his arm? If only he could get a flight out and catch up with her.

Fortunately, the weather was cooperative and the highway traffic, though heavy, wasn't as bad as the last time he'd made this trip. He got to the airport before noon, and after securing a standby ticket on a late-night flight to Phoenix, he searched the departure board for other flights headed for Arizona. After racing to a gate where the airline Gillian had mentioned was scheduled to take off for Phoenix, he realized he was too late. The plane was already boarded and just backing out. She was probably on it.

Feeling like he was about to embark on a fool's mission, he turned to leave. Then he noticed a slender girl with sleek black hair slowly walking away. She looked weary and dejected, her shoulders slumped, and her carry-on bag trailing behind her.

"Emma!" he called out. When she turned, he knew it was her. But her expression, after recovering from the shock, was a mixture of dismay and irritation.

"What are you doing here?" she asked.

"Trying to get a flight to Phoenix." He studied her troubled face. Had he misread her feelings toward him yesterday? Or was she upset over discovering his identity?

"Good luck with that." She nodded toward the gate. "I had a standby ticket on that flight but turns out they were booked full. Actually, overbooked."

"Oh." He nodded. "I got a standby ticket too."

"So you're going to spend Christmas with your family at the Landerses' Scottsdale house?" She pushed her hair behind her shoulders.

"I guess so." He tried to think of a way to express himself, but he felt tongue-tied.

"Well, I don't want to keep you from —"

"Emma," he began slowly. "I didn't come

193

here because I want to go to Scottsdale to be with my family. I came here because of *you.*"

She looked up with misty dark eyes. *"Why?"*

"Because I, uh, I do care about you." For some reason, he wasn't ready to declare his full love quite yet. Not like this in the overly crowded airport with curious onlookers milling about.

"You care about me?" She tilted her head to one side. "Then why did you keep me in the dark about who you really are, West? Why did you make me believe you were the caretaker of the house? Why did you trick me?"

"It's a long story." He glanced around the busy terminal. "But I'd like a chance to explain . . . and apologize."

"Well, I've got plenty of time. The next standby flight isn't until this evening."

"Then why not forget about it?"

"Forget about what?" She looked confused.

"Don't go home to Arizona, Emma. Come back to Breckenridge with me. *Please.*"

"No." She firmly shook her head. "I can't do that."

"Please, Emma, I'm begging you to come back. I'm so sorry I didn't tell you about who I —"

"But you told Gillian," she said. "All this time she knew who you were, and I was completely oblivious. Do you know how that made me feel?"

"I can imagine. But you have to understand — I never told Gillian —"

"I guess it explains why Gillian was suddenly over the moon for you. But I can't believe you let the rest of us go on thinking you —"

"I didn't mean for it to go like that. And you have to believe me, I never told Gillian anything. She figured that out for herself. I had my suspicions she was onto me, but when I confronted her, she totally denied it." Just then Emma was nearly knocked over by a fast-walking group of people. West caught her by the hand. "Let's go somewhere quieter to talk."

As he led her through the bustling terminal, he realized there was no quiet, private spot. So he led her toward baggage claim, hoping he'd be able to convince her to return to Breckenridge.

"I suspect that neither of us is going to get a standby seat," he said as they navigated the crowds. "Let's just go back to Breckenridge before it's too late and we're both stuck here for the night."

"I just want to go home." Her voice trembled with emotion as they stopped by the escalator. "I want to go home."

"I know, Emma. I get that. But what if you can't get a flight? And there's weather predicted. We could get a big dump of snow by —"

"Will that affect flights?"

"It could." He reached for her bag. "Come back to Breckenridge, Emma. If you don't want me around, I promise to hole up in my studio until you and the Landerses go back to Arizona."

"So the place you called the caretaker's cottage — that's really your studio?" she asked. "Just like Gillian said?"

"Well, it was a caretaker's cottage when I bought the place," he said. "But I turned it into a music studio."

"And you told Gillian about that too."

"No, I swear to you, I never told Gillian anything personal about myself. She figured it out on her own. And I've wanted to confess the truth to you, Emma." He paused to look into her eyes. "I tried to last night — a couple of times — but we got interrupted."

"But why did you have to trick me in the first place?" she demanded. "Why pretend to be something you're not, West? It's like

196

everything I knew about you was a big fat lie." She had tears in her eyes now.

"If you come back home with me, I will explain everything to you. I promise."

Emma bit her lip with a creased brow.

"Just trust me, Emma." He reached for her hand. "You don't want to spend Christmas here at the airport with a bunch of strangers."

She sighed. "I guess that's true."

"So come on, give me a chance to explain."

She pursed her lips.

"If we leave right now, you might even be able to get in a few ski runs before the lifts close today. Christmas Eve skiing . . . it could be fun."

Her eyes brightened slightly. "Really? People ski on Christmas Eve?"

"You bet." He patted her back. "Come on, Emma, let's go home."

As glad as she'd been to see West — at first — Emma still questioned whether she'd given in too easily. But the idea of spending Christmas Eve in Denver International Airport wasn't exactly inviting. Especially when she already felt so tired. But as West drove his Jeep out of the airport, Emma was plagued with second thoughts. Had she simply set herself up for more heartache? What about her resolve last night — to simply disappear and be done with him for good. And Gillian as well!

It just made no sense. Why would someone as successful and wealthy as TW Prescott want to waste his time on a lowly substitute teacher with missionary parents? It was different when West, the kind caretaker, had taken an interest in her. That seemed a more level playing field. But TW Prescott, the successful songwriter? Well, that just boggled her mind. Still, she wanted to sort this thing out.

"Okay," she began slowly. "How about you start telling me why you decided to deceive me like that. Was it just a joke? A game? Like something Gillian might do?"

"Ouch." He grimaced. "But I suppose I deserve to be compared to Gillian."

"Yeah. Maybe you guys aren't such opposites after all."

"Ouch again."

She sighed. "Sorry . . . well, sort of. Gillian isn't all bad. And I'm sure you're not either. I'm just very, very confused, West."

"Right. That's why I want to explain. Let me start at the beginning." He explained how his mother and stepfather had decided a house swap for Christmas was a good idea. "But I didn't want to go to Arizona for Christmas."

"I guess I can't blame you for that. I wouldn't trade your place for the Landerses' house either. Especially at Christmastime. Even so . . ."

"Yeah . . . anyway, I met Gillian that first day and she started grilling me, asking what I was doing — at my own house. I didn't want to admit that I lived there, so I made up the stupid story about being the caretaker. And in a way, it's not a total lie. I do take care of my house. I mean, I hire help too. But it's mostly up to me. That's how I like it."

"Okay, I can sort of understand you not wanting Gillian to know who you were. But what was the point in keeping your little charade going? Especially with me? I thought that we . . . well, that we had something more."

"We did have something more. I hope we still do. Or that we still will after I help you understand." He told her about other relationships he'd had with women, ones who had been more attracted to his name and bank account than to him.

"Kinda like Gillian."

"Case in point." He nodded vigorously.

"And you thought I'd be like *that*?" She

couldn't keep the hurt out of her voice.

"No, I didn't. Not at first. But then I thought you'd dropped me for Harris. And then I wasn't so sure."

"That was Gillian's doing."

"Yes. We figured that out. I wanted to tell you about who I am, Emma. I started to tell you."

"But you got interrupted." She did remember a moment or two when he'd seemed about to say something important. "So, okay, I get why you did that at first . . . and how you got stuck in that role. But it doesn't answer all my questions."

"Then ask away. I have nothing to hide. I want to be an open book for you."

She thought hard. "Maybe it's not questions so much. It's more like concerns."

"Well, go ahead and voice them, Emma. I can take it."

Now she didn't know what to say. She'd already been so wrong about him . . . believing he was the caretaker . . . What if she'd been wrong to assume his feelings for her were along the same lines as her feelings? Was she a fool to imagine he was interested in a committed relationship? After only knowing her a few days? Wasn't that totally ridiculous? In all likelihood, he was simply a rich guy looking for a holiday fling. Have some fun with the Arizona girls then send them packing? No biggie.

"Come on," he urged. "Tell me your concerns."

"Oh, I don't know. Maybe it doesn't matter."

"Well, it matters to me."

"Okay then." She took in a deep breath. "Well, you sort of led me to think you were interested in me."

"I *am* interested. Haven't I made that clear?"

"Maybe . . . but for some reason it was easier for me to take your interest more seriously when you were the caretaker."

"Aha." He nodded with a knowing expression. "Meaning you could fall for a lowly caretaker, but not for TW Prescott?"

"We live in different worlds, West. I'm a substitute teacher who's trying to break into music, and you're —"

"You're actually a very talented musician, Emma."

"Of course, you'd say that."

"No, I mean it. I don't toss praise around lightly. I mean, sure, you're not very experienced, but you've definitely got talent."

"Well, thanks . . . I think."

"So, let me get this clear. You think that because of my success, I wouldn't be seriously interested in you?"

"Something like that." Emma sighed. "I guess I'm just generally confused — and incredibly tired. Last night, after it felt like you pulled the rug out from under me, well, I couldn't sleep at all. I finally got up and packed my bags and cleaned my room — which I'm guessing is actually your room."

"Yeah."

"Anyway, I knew I wanted to go home. I stayed up and waited until six to call a taxi. And I'm so exhausted right now, I can't even think straight."

"Then lean your seat back and take a nap." He reached into the back seat for a fleece blanket, tossing it onto her.

"The drive is more than an hour from here. We can talk when we get home."

Home, she thought as she closed her eyes. *Where was home?* In Tempe where she lived by herself? In Uganda with her parents? In Scottsdale with Gillian and her family? Maybe Emma was destined to never have a real home.

West didn't mind that Emma slept the rest of the way home. In a way, it was comforting to see her peacefully lying there. He'd glance her way every once in a while, to reassure himself she was truly here with him.

Each time he'd be filled with a protective feeling for her. He never wanted her to be hurt again. Not by him or anyone.

It wasn't until he rolled into town that she began to stir. "Wake up, Sleeping Beauty," he said. "We're home."

"Oh." She sat up and looked around. "That was fast."

He chuckled. "For you anyway. Where do you want to go? Are you hungry? Ready to ski?"

"Both, actually."

"You're still up for skiing?"

"Isn't that how you enticed me to come back with you? The temptation of snow and skiing?"

"Great. We'll go get our gear, pack up a bite to eat, and —"

"Only I don't want to go into the house. I'm not ready to see Gillian just yet."

"Then we can sneak into my studio. I've got food there. I'll load up our stuff and we'll be on the mountain in time for an hour or so of skiing before the lifts close. I don't know about you, but I can't think of a better way to spend Christmas Eve."

"Maybe I should text Gillian . . . let her know that I'm coming back." Emma pulled out her phone. "That way they won't be too surprised when I show up after we're done skiing."

"Yeah, I think they were pretty worried about you." He explained how Gillian had come over to tip him off this morning. "And she even apologized."

"Seriously? Did it seem sincere?"

"I think so." He pulled right up to the studio, and not seeing anyone around, they hopped out and hurried inside. "Sorry about the mess." He tossed some discarded clothing toward a hamper. "I left in a rush this morning."

But Emma stood in front of the small fireplace, staring at the music awards lining the mantle. "Wow, this is impressive, West. And intimidating."

"Yeah, I feel like that sometimes too."

She tried not to roll her eyes. "Right, you're intimidated by your own awards."

"You'd be surprised." He went over to the kitchenette, poking in the fridge.

"How about I fix us something while you load up the skis?" she offered.

"Great idea. And it'll save time if we take it with us and eat up there." He handed her a daypack. "Go ahead and put some things in here. I'll be right back."

It wasn't long before they were riding a chair up to an intermediate run. West had taken his sister and nephews up this slope before and knew of a nice resting stop, tucked away about halfway down. It would be just right for their dinner . . . and if the timing seemed right, maybe even something more.

When he led Emma off the main run, turning onto a wooded side trail, she grew curious. "Where are you going?" she asked.

"It's a surprise." He led her over to the clearing, brushing the snow off a boulder to create a sturdy bench. "How about a picnic here?"

"Perfect." She sat down. "I'm starving."

"So what did you make for us?" He removed the daypack and opened it, extracting a bag of chips.

"Turkey and Swiss cheese sandwiches," she said.

"My favorite." He removed a couple of bruised bananas. "And fresh fruit."

"Not terribly fresh. They looked better when I packed them. And, no offense, but the pickings were a little slim in your kitchen."

"You're telling me. But this feels like a regular little feast to me." He took a bite of his sandwich. "Perfect!" They continued to visit as they ate. Emma had a few more questions for him, but he could tell she was slowly adjusting herself to last night's revelations. Finally they were done and he tucked the remnants back into his pack before moving closer to her.

"Thanks for making us such a great meal." He turned to look at her. "Especially considering what you had to work with."

"I'm used to making ends meet." She smiled at him.

"So, tell me the truth, Emma. Can a girl like you be interested in a guy like me? I mean, now that you know who I really am. Or does it make you want to turn and run the other way?" He sighed. "Well, I guess that's pretty much what you did today . . . you ran the other way."

"I won't deny I was overwhelmed . . . and hurt."

He nodded. "I feel bad that I hurt you." He reached into his jacket pocket for the folded paper he'd slipped in earlier. "I wrote a song for you."

"You're kidding. For me?" She blinked.

"Yeah. I couldn't sleep last night either. I felt so bad about the way you learned the truth, when I had wanted to tell you myself."

"Are you going to sing it?"

He chuckled. "I might not sound too good without accompaniment to keep me on tune."

206

"That's okay. I'd still like to hear it."

And so he sang it to her. It was a simple song . . . an expression of love for his dark-haired girl with a sparkle in her eyes and kindness in her voice. He could tell by her smile that she liked it. When he finished and leaned in to kiss her, she leaned in too. That's when he knew that a girl like her could love a guy like him. Simply for himself.

After they exchanged a few more kisses, he could feel her shivering.

"You're cold." He stood. "We should get moving." He helped her back into her skis then led her toward the run, both of them pausing at the crest of the hill.

"Ready, set, go," she said in a teasing tone.

He knew she didn't want to race but decided to make it seem like he was racing her — only he'd let her win. They were almost to the bottom — with Emma just barely ahead — when she suddenly took a sharp turn and barreled straight into him. In a tangled mess of skis and poles, arms and legs, they tumbled into the snow.

"Are you okay?" he asked when they finally quit sliding, coming to rest on the side of the nearly vacant run.

"Other than being embarrassed, I'm just fine." She laughed. "How about you?"

"I'm okay." He grinned and, tugging her to a sitting position beside him, pointed westward. "Look, we're just in time for the sunset."

"With a front-row seat."

He put his arm around her, pulling her closer in hopes of keeping her warm — and near. "The lifts are all closed now. Everyone is calling it a day."

"Look how pretty the lodge looks with its lights reflecting off the snow. Just like a picture." She sighed happily. "What a perfect Christmas."

"Almost."

"Almost?" She turned to look at him. "How could it possibly be better?"

"Emma." He turned around to face her now, determined to take this big step.

"What?" Her dark eyes opened wide.

West knew he had caught her off guard. Was he moving too fast? And yet . . . . deep inside he knew this was right. Something inside of him had clicked into place — almost as soon as they'd first met.

"Are you okay?" she asked.

He realized he probably looked ridiculous, just staring into her eyes like this. "I realize we haven't known each other for long. Not by the usual standards, anyway."

"That's true." She nodded. "But I do feel

like I know you, West. I'm not even sure how it happened."

"That's exactly how I feel. I can't even explain it, but it's something I don't want to let slip away."

She smiled shyly. "I don't either."

"In fact, that's why I stayed around home instead of joining my family in Arizona. I wanted to get to know you."

"I'm glad you stayed."

"But now I'm counting the days until you and the Landerses will be leaving." He frowned. "And that worries me."

"It worries you?" She tipped her head to one side. "I thought you'd be glad to have your house back."

"Yeah, that's true. But I don't want to see you leave so soon, Emma."

She seemed to consider this. "What if I stuck around longer? It's not like I have anything to get back to right away."

"That'd be great!" He enthusiastically hugged her, almost making them tumble down the slope, but he dug his heels into the snow to anchor them.

"I'm not sure what the Landerses will think." She grinned. "But I'm not sure it matters."

"Not to me." He pulled her closer to him.

"Maybe my skiing will improve too." Her

eyes sparkled.

"No doubt about that." He watched a snowflake drift down and land gracefully on her nose. Leaning in to flick it off, he moved closer for a kiss. A kiss that she warmly returned, assuring him that her feelings really did align with his.

She smiled. "This place is so beautiful, West. No wonder you make your home here."

"And it's not just a Christmas town," he assured her.

"But it is pretty special at Christmas." She paused to watch a couple of snowboarders whiz past.

When she turned back around, he used the opportunity to kiss her again. "Merry Christmas, Emma."

"Merry Christmas!" She gave him a slightly worried look. "It won't be easy telling the Landerses that I won't be going home with them."

"Don't worry. I'll help you with that." He helped her to stand, embracing her again. "You're right, Emma. It's really going to be a perfect Christmas!"

ABOUT THE AUTHOR

With around 250 books published and 7.5 million sold, **Melody Carlson** is one of the most prolific writers of our times. Writing primarily for women and teens, and in various genres, she has won numerous national awards — including the Rita, Gold Medallion, Carol Award, Christy, and two career achievement awards. Several of her novels have been optioned for film, and her first Hallmark movie, *All Summer Long,* premiered in 2019. Melody makes her home in the Pacific Northwest, where she lives with her husband near the Cascade Mountains. When not writing, Melody enjoys interior design, gardening, camping, and biking.

The employees of Thorndike Press hope you have enjoyed this Large Print book. All our Thorndike, Wheeler, and Kennebec Large Print titles are designed for easy reading, and all our books are made to last. Other Thorndike Press Large Print books are available at your library, through selected bookstores, or directly from us.

For information about titles, please call:
  (800) 223-1244

or visit our website at:
  gale.com/thorndike

To share your comments, please write:
  Publisher
  Thorndike Press
  10 Water St., Suite 310
  Waterville, ME 04901